Bernard Mac Laverty

A TIME TO DANCE

and other stories

VINTAGE

Published by Vintage 1999

8 10 9

First published in Great Britain in 1982
by Jonathan Cape

Vintage
Random House, 20 Vauxhall Bridge Road,
London SW1V 2SA

Random House Australia (Pty) Limited
20 Alfred Street, Milsons Point, Sydney
New South Wales 2061, Australia

Random House New Zealand Limited
18 Poland Road, Glenfield, Auckland 10,
New Zealand

Random House (Pty) Limited
Endulini, 5a Jubilee Road, Parktown 2193,
South Africa

The Random House Group Limited Reg. No. 954009
www.randomhouse.co.uk

A CIP catalogue record for this book
is available from the British Library

ISBN 978 0 09 928356 0

Penguin Random House is committed to a sustainable future for
our business, our readers and our planet. This book is made from
Forest Stewardship Council® certified paper.

Printed and bound in Great Britain by Clays Ltd, St Ives plc

For my mother

Contents

Acknowledgments

The following stories in this collection appeared previously, as listed: The Beginnings of a Sin (*In Dublin*, 1981); Father and Son (*Scottish Short Stories*, Collins, 1978); Life Drawing (*Firebird I*, Penguin, 1982); My Dear Palestrina (B.B.C. Radio 4, 1980; B.B.C. Television, 1980); Phonefun Limited (Glasgow Theatre Club, Tron Theatre, 1981; B.B.C. Radio, Northern Ireland, 1982); A Time to Dance (*Scottish Short Stories*, Collins, 1980).

The author and publishers are grateful to A.T.V. Music Ltd for permission to quote the extract from the song 'Two Brothers' by Irving Gordon on pp. 32–3.

Father and Son

BECAUSE I DO not sleep well I hear my father rising
to go to work. I know that in a few minutes he will
come in to look at me sleeping. He will want to
check that I came home last night. He will stand in his bare
feet, his shoes and socks in his hand, looking at me. I will
sleep for him. Downstairs I hear the snap of the switch on the
kettle. I hear him not eating anything, going about the
kitchen with a stomach full of wind. He will come again to
look at me before he goes out to his work. He will want a
conversation. He climbs the stairs and stands breathing
through his nose with an empty lunch box in the crook of his
arm, looking at me.

This is my son who let me down. I love him so much it hurts
but he won't talk to me. He tells me nothing. I hear him
groan and see his eyes flicker open. When he sees me he turns
away, a heave of bedclothes in his wake.

'Wake up, son. I'm away to my work. Where are you going
today?'
  'What's it to you?'
  'If I know what you're doing I don't worry as much.'
  'Shit.'

9

I do not sleep. My father does not sleep. The sound of ambulances criss-crosses the dark. I sleep with the daylight. It is safe. At night I hear his bare feet click as he lifts them, walking the lino. The front door shudders as he leaves.

My son is breaking my heart. It is already broken. Is it my fault there is no woman in the house? Is it my fault a good woman should die? His face was never softer than when after I had shaved. A baby pressed to my shaved cheek. Now his chin is sandpaper. He is a man. When he was a boy I took him fishing. I taught him how to tie a blood-knot, how to cast a fly, how to strike so the fish would not escape. How to play a fish. The green bus to quiet days in Toome. Him pestering me with questions. If I leave him alone he will break my heart anyway. I must speak to him. Tonight at tea. If he is in.

'You should be in your bed. A man of your age. It's past one.'
   'Let me make you some tea.'
   The boy shrugs and sits down. He takes up the paper between him and his father.
   'What do you be doing out to this time?'
   'Not again.'
   'Answer me.'
   'Talking.'
   'Who with?'
   'Friends. Just go to bed, Da, will you?'
   'What do you talk about?'
   'Nothing much.'
   'Talk to me, son.'
   'What about?'

My son, he looks confused. I want you to talk to me the way I hear you talk to people at the door. I want to hear you laugh with me like you used to. I want to know what you think. I want to know why you do not eat more. No more than pickings for four weeks. Your face is thin. Your fingers, orange with nicotine. I pulled you away from death once and now you will not talk to me. I want to know if you are in danger again.

'About . . .'
   'You haven't shaved yet.'
   'I'm just going to. The water in the kettle is hot.'
   'Why do you shave at night?'
   'Because in the morning my hand shakes.'

Your hand shakes in the morning, Da, because you're a coward. You think the world is waiting round the corner to blow your head off. A breakfast of two Valium and the rest of them rattling in your pocket, walking down the street to your work. Won't answer the door without looking out the bedroom window first. He's scared of his own shadow.

Son, you are living on borrowed time. Your hand shook when you got home. I have given you the life you now have. I fed you soup from a spoon when your own hand would have spilled it. Let me put my arm around your shoulders and let me listen to what is making you thin. At the weekend I will talk to him.

It is hard to tell if his bed has been slept in. It is always rumpled. I have not seen my son for two days. Then, on the radio, I hear he is dead. They give out his description. I drink milk. I cry.
   But he comes in for his tea.

'Why don't you tell me where you are?'
   'Because I never know where I am.'

My mother is dead but I have another one in her place. He is an old woman. He has been crying. I know he prays for me all the time. He used to dig the garden, grow vegetables and flowers for half the street. He used to fish. To take me fishing. Now he just waits. He sits and waits for me and the weeds have taken over. I would like to slap his face and make a man out of him.

'I let you go once – and look what happened.'
　'Not this again.'
The boy curls his lip as if snagged on a fish-hook.

For two years I never heard a scrape from you. I read of London in the papers. Watched scenes from London on the news, looking over the reporter's shoulder at people walking in the street. I know you, son, you are easily led. Then a doctor phoned for me at work. The poshest man I ever spoke to.

　'I had to go and collect you. Like a dog.'
The boy had taken up a paper. He turns the pages noisily, crackling like fire.

　'A new rig-out from Littlewoods.'
Socks, drawers, shirt, the lot. In a carrier bag. The doctor said he had to burn what was on you. I made you have your girl's hair cut. It was Belfast before we spoke. You had the taint of England in your voice.

　'Today I thought you were dead.'

Every day you think I am dead. You live in fear. Of your own death. Peeping behind curtains, the radio always loud enough to drown any noise that might frighten you, double locking doors. When you think I am not looking you hold your stomach. You undress in the dark for fear of your shadow falling on the window-blind. At night you lie with the pillow over your head. By your bed a hatchet which you pretend to have forgotten to tidy away. Mice have more courage.

'Well I'm not dead.'

'Why don't you tell me where you go?'

'Look, Da, I have not touched the stuff since I came back. Right?'

'Why don't you have a girl like everybody else?'

'Oh fuck.'

He bundles the paper and hurls it in the corner and stamps up the stairs to his room. The old man shouts at the closed door.

'Go and wash your mouth out.'

He cries again, staring at the ceiling so that the tears run down to his ears.

My son, he is full of hatred. For me, for everything. He spits when he speaks. When he shouts his voice breaks high and he is like a woman. He grinds his teeth and his skin goes white about his mouth. His hands shake. All because I ask him where he goes. Perhaps I need to show him more love. Care for him more than I do.

I mount the stairs quietly to apologise. My son, I am sorry. I do it because I love you. Let me put my arm around you and talk like we used to on the bus from Toome. Why do you fight away from me?

The door swings open and he pushes a hand-gun beneath the pillow. Seen long enough, black and squat, dull like a garden slug. He sits, my son, his hands idling empty, staring hatred.

'Why do you always spy on me, you nosey old bastard?' His voice breaks, his eyes bulge.

'What's that? Under your pillow?'

'It's none of your fucking business.'

He kicks the door closed in my face with his bare foot.

I am in the dark of the landing. I must pray for him. On my bended knees I will pray for him to be safe. Perhaps I did not

13

see what I saw. Maybe I am mistaken. My son rides pillion on a motor-bike. Tonight I will not sleep. I do not think I will sleep again.

It is ten o'clock. The news begins. Like a woman I stand drying a plate, watching the headlines. There is a ring at the door. The boy answers it, his shirt-tail out. Voices in the hallway.

My son with friends. Talking. What he does not do with me.

There is a bang. A dish-cloth drops from my hand and I run to the kitchen door. Not believing, I look into the hallway. There is a strange smell. My son is lying on the floor, his head on the bottom stair, his feet on the threshold. The news has come to my door. The house is open to the night. There is no one else. I go to him with damp hands.

'Are you hurt?'

Blood is spilling from his nose.

They have punched you and you are not badly hurt. Your nose is bleeding. Something cold at the back of your neck.

I take my son's limp head in my hands and see a hole in his nose that should not be there. At the base of his nostril.

My son, let me put my arms around you.

A Time to Dance

NELSON, WITH A patch over one eye, stood looking idly into Mothercare's window. The sun was bright behind him and made a mirror out of the glass. He looked at his patch with distaste and felt it with his finger. The Elastoplast was rough and dry and he disliked the feel of it. Bracing himself for the pain, he ripped it off and let a yell out of him. A woman looked down at him curiously to see why he had made the noise, but by that time he had the patch in his pocket. He knew without looking that some of his eyebrow would be on it.

He had spent most of the morning in the Gardens avoiding distant uniforms, but now that it was coming up to lunchtime he braved it on to the street. He had kept his patch on longer than usual because his mother had told him the night before that if he didn't wear it he would go 'stark, staring blind'.

Nelson was worried because he knew what it was like to be blind. The doctor at the eye clinic had given him a box of patches that would last for most of his lifetime. Opticludes. One day Nelson had worn two and tried to get to the end of the street and back. It was a terrible feeling. He had to hold his head back in case it bumped into anything and keep waving his hands in front of him backwards and forwards like windscreen wipers. He kept tramping on tin cans and heard

15

them trundle emptily away. Broken glass crackled under his feet and he could not figure out how close to the wall he was. Several times he heard footsteps approaching, slowing down as if they were going to attack him in his helplessness, then walking away. One of the footsteps even laughed. Then he heard a voice he knew only too well.

'Jesus, Nelson, what are you up to this time?' It was his mother. She led him back to the house with her voice blaring in his ear.

She was always shouting. Last night, for instance, she had started into him for watching T.V. from the side. She had dragged him round to the chair in front of it.

'That's the way the manufacturers make the sets. They put the picture on the front. But oh no, that's not good enough for our Nelson. He has to watch it from the side. Squint, my arse, you'll just go blind – stark, staring blind.'

Nelson had then turned his head and watched it from the front. She had never mentioned the blindness before. Up until now all she had said was, 'If you don't wear them patches that eye of yours will turn in till it's looking at your brains. God knows, not that it'll have much to look at.'

His mother was Irish. That was why she had a name like Skelly. That was why she talked funny. But she was proud of the way she talked and nothing angered her more than to hear Nelson saying 'Ah ken' and 'What like is it?' She kept telling him that someday they were going back, when she had enough ha'pence scraped together. 'Until then I'll not let them make a Scotchman out of you.' But Nelson talked the way he talked.

His mother had called him Nelson because she said she thought that his father had been a seafaring man. The day the boy was born she had read an article in the *Reader's Digest* about Nelson Rockefeller, one of the richest men in the world. It seemed only right to give the boy a good start. She

thought it also had the advantage that it couldn't be short-
ened, but she was wrong. Most of the boys in the scheme
called him Nelly Skelly.

He wondered if he should sneak back to school for dinner
then skive off again in the afternoon. They had good dinners
at school – like a hotel, with choices. Chips and magic things
like rhubarb crumble. There was one big dinner-woman who
gave him extra every time she saw him. She told him he
needed fattening. The only drawback to the whole system
was that he was on free dinners. Other people in his class were
given their dinner money and it was up to them whether they
went without a dinner and bought Coke and sweets and stuff
with the money. It was a choice Nelson didn't have, so he had
to invent other things to get the money out of his mother. In
Lent there were the Black Babies; library fines were worth the
odd 10p, although, as yet, he had not taken a book from the
school library – and anyway they didn't have to pay fines,
even if they were late; the Home Economics Department
asked them to bring in money to buy their ingredients and
Nelson would always add 20p to it.

'What the hell are they teaching you to cook – sides of
beef?' his mother would yell. Outdoor pursuits required
extra money. But even though they had ended after the
second term, Nelson went on asking for the 50p on a Friday –
'to go horse riding'. His mother would never part with
money without a speech of some sort.

'Horse riding? Horse riding! Jesus, I don't know what sort
of a school I've sent you to. Is Princess Anne in your class or
something? Holy God, horse riding.'

Outdoor pursuits was mostly walking round museums on
wet days and, when it was dry, the occasional trip to Porto-
bello beach to write on a flapping piece of foolscap the signs of
pollution you could see. Nelson felt that the best outdoor
pursuit of the lot was what he was doing now. Skiving. At
least that way you could do what you liked.

He groped in his pocket for the change out of his 50p and went into a shop. He bought a giant thing of bubble-gum and crammed it into his mouth. It was hard and dry at first and he couldn't answer the woman when she spoke to him.

'Whaaungh?'

'Pick the paper off the floor, son! Use the basket.'

He picked the paper up and screwed it into a ball. He aimed to miss the basket, just to spite her, but it went in. By the time he reached the bottom of the street the gum was chewy. He thrust his tongue into the middle of it and blew. A small disappointing bubble burst with a plip. It was not until the far end of Princes Street that he managed to blow big ones, pink and wobbling, that he could see at the end of his nose, which burst well and had to be gathered in shreds from his chin.

Then suddenly the crowds of shoppers parted and he saw his mother. In the same instant she saw him. She was on him before he could even think of running. She grabbed him by the fur of his parka and began screaming into his face.

'In the name of God, Nelson, what are you doing here? Why aren't you at school?' She began shaking him. 'Do you realise what this means? They'll put me in bloody jail. It'll be bloody Saughton for me, and no mistake.' She had her teeth gritted together and her mouth was slanting in her face. Then Nelson started to shout.

'Help! Help!' he yelled.

A woman with an enormous chest like a pigeon stopped. 'What's happening?' she said.

Nelson's mother turned on her. 'It's none of your bloody business.'

'I'm being kidnapped,' yelled Nelson.

'Young woman. Young woman . . . ' said the lady with the large chest, trying to tap Nelson's mother on the shoulder with her umbrella, but Mrs Skelly turned with such a snarl that the woman edged away hesitatingly and looked over her

18

shoulder and tut-tutted just loudly enough for the passing crowd to hear her.

'Help! I'm being kidnapped,' screamed Nelson, but everybody walked past looking the other way. His mother squatted down in front of him, still holding on to his jacket. She lowered her voice and tried to make it sound reasonable.

'Look Nelson, love. Listen. If you're skiving school, do you realise what'll happen to me? In Primary the Children's Panel threatened to send me to court. You're only at that Secondary and already that Sub-Attendance Committee thing wanted to fine me. Jesus, if you're caught again . . . '

Nelson stopped struggling. The change in her tone had quietened him down. She straightened up and looked wildly about her, wondering what to do.

'You've got to go straight back to school, do you hear me?'

'Yes.'

'Promise me you'll go.' The boy looked down at the ground. 'Promise?' The boy made no answer.

'I'll kill you if you don't go back. I'd take you myself only I've my work to go to. I'm late as it is.'

Again she looked around as if she would see someone who would suddenly help her. Still she held on to his jacket. She was biting her lip.

'Oh God, Nelson.'

The boy blew a flesh-pink bubble and snapped it between his teeth. She shook him.

'That bloody bubble-gum.'

There was a loud explosion as the one o'clock gun went off. They both leapt.

'Oh Jesus, that gun puts the heart sideways in me every time it goes off. Come on, son, you'll have to come with me. I'm late. I don't know what they'll say when they see you but I'm bloody taking you to school by the ear. You hear me?'

She began rushing along the street, Nelson's sleeve in one

hand, her carrier bag in the other. The boy had to run to keep from being dragged.

'Don't you dare try a trick like that again. Kidnapped, my arse. Nelson, if I knew somebody who would kidnap you – I'd pay *him* the money. Embarrassing me on the street like that.'

They turned off the main road and went into a hallway and up carpeted stairs which had full-length mirrors along one side. Nelson stopped to make faces at himself but his mother chugged at his arm. At the head of the stairs stood a fat man in his shirtsleeves.

'What the hell is this?' he said. 'You're late, and what the hell is that?' He looked down from over his stomach at Nelson.

'I'll explain later,' she said. 'I'll make sure he stays in the room.'

'You should be on *now*,' said the fat man and turned and walked away through the swing doors. They followed him and Nelson saw, before his mother pushed him into the room, that it was a bar, plush and carpeted with crowds of men standing drinking.

'You sit here, Nelson, until I'm finished and then I'm taking you back to that school. You'll get nowhere if you don't do your lessons. I have to get changed now.'

She set her carrier bag on the floor and kicked off her shoes. Nelson sat down, watching her. She stopped and looked over her shoulder at him, biting her lip.

'Where's that bloody eyepatch you should be wearing?' Nelson indicated his pocket.

'Well, wear it then.' Nelson took the crumpled patch from his pocket, tugging bits of it unstuck to get it flat before he stuck it over his bad eye. His mother took out her handbag and began rooting about at the bottom of it. Nelson heard the rattle of her bottles of scent and tubes of lipstick.

'Ah,' she said and produced another eyepatch, flicking it

clean. 'Put another one on till I get changed. I don't want you noseying at me.' She came to him, pulling away the white backing to the patch, and stuck it over his remaining eye. He imagined her concentrating, the tip of her tongue stuck out. She pressed his eyebrows with her thumbs, making sure that the patches were stuck.

'Now don't move, or you'll bump into something.'

Nelson heard the slither of her clothes and her small grunts as she hurriedly got changed. Then he heard her rustle in her bag, the soft pop and rattle as she opened her capsules. Her 'tantalisers' she called them, small black and red torpedoes. Then he heard her voice.

'Just you stay like that till I come back. That way you'll come to no harm. You hear me, Nelson? If I come back in here and you have those things off, I'll *kill* you. I'll not be long.'

Nelson nodded from his darkness.

'The door will be locked, so there's no running away.'

'Ah ken.'

Suddenly his darkness exploded with lights as he felt her bony hand strike his ear.

'You don't ken things, Nelson. You *know* them.'

He heard her go out and the key turn in the lock. His ear sang and he felt it was hot. He turned his face up to the ceiling. She had left the light on because he could see pinkish through the patches. He smelt the beer and stale smoke. Outside the room pop music had started up, very loudly. He heard the deep notes pound through to where he sat. He felt his ear with his hand and it *was* hot.

Making small *aww* sounds of excruciating pain, he slowly detached both eyepatches from the bridge of the nose outwards. In case his mother should come back he did not take them off completely, but left them hinged to the sides of his eyes. When he turned to look around him they flapped like blinkers.

It wasn't really a room, more a broom cupboard. Crates were stacked against one wall; brushes and mops and buckets stood near a very low sink; on a row of coat-hooks hung some limp raincoats and stained white jackets; his mother's stuff hung on the last hook. The floor was covered with tramped-flat cork tips. Nelson got up to look at what he was sitting on. It was a crate of empties. He went to the keyhole and looked out, but all he could see was a patch of wallpaper opposite. Above the door was a narrow window. He looked up at it, his eyepatches falling back to touch his ears. He went over to the sink and had a drink of water from the low tap, sucking noisily at the column of water as it splashed into the sink. He stopped and wiped his mouth. The water felt cold after the mint of the bubble-gum. He looked up at his mother's things, hanging on the hook; her tights and drawers were as she wore them, but inside out and hanging knock-kneed on top of everything. In her bag he found her blonde wig and tried it on, smelling the perfume of it as he did so. At home he liked noseying in his mother's room; smelling all her bottles of make-up; seeing her spangled things. He had to stand on the crate to see himself but the mirror was all brown measles under its surface and the eyepatches ruined the effect. He sat down again and began pulling at the bubble-gum, seeing how long he could make it stretch before it broke. Still the music pounded outside. It was so loud the vibrations tickled his feet. He sighed and looked up at the window again.

If his mother took him back to school, he could see problems. For starting St John the Baptist's she had bought him a brand new Adidas bag for his books. Over five pounds it had cost her, she said. On his first real skive he had dumped the bag in the bin at the bottom of his stair, every morning for a week, and travelled light into town. On the Friday he came home just in time to see the bin lorry driving away in a cloud of bluish smoke. He had told his mother that the bag

22

had been stolen from the playground during break. She had threatened to phone the school about it but Nelson had hastily assured her that the whole matter was being investigated by none other than the Headmaster himself. This threat put the notion out of his head of asking her for the money to replace the books. At that point he had not decided on a figure. He could maybe try it again some time when all the fuss had died down. But now it was all going to be stirred if his mother took him to school.

He pulled two crates to the door and climbed up but they were not high enough. He put a third one on top, climbed on again, and gingerly straightened, balancing on its rim. On tip-toe he could see out. He couldn't see his mother anywhere. He saw a crowd of men standing in a semicircle. Behind them were some very bright lights, red, yellow and blue. They all had pints in their hands which they didn't seem to be drinking. They were all watching something which Nelson couldn't see. Suddenly the music stopped and the men all began drinking and talking. Standing on tip-toe for so long, Nelson's legs began to shake and he heard the bottles in the crate rattle. He rested for a moment. Then the music started again. He looked to see. The men now just stood looking. It was as if they were seeing a ghost. Then they all cheered louder than the music.

Nelson climbed down and put the crates away from the door so that his mother could get in. He closed his eyepatches over for a while, but still she didn't come. He listened to another record, this time a slow one. He decided to travel blind to get another drink of water. As he did so the music changed to fast. He heard the men cheering again, then the rattle of the key in the lock. Nelson, his arms rotating in front of him, tried to make his way back to the crate. His mother's voice said,

'Don't you dare take those eyepatches off.' Her voice was panting. Then his hand hit up against her. It was her bare stomach, hot and damp with sweat. She guided him to sit down, breathing heavily through her nose.

'I'll just get changed and then you're for school right away, boy.' Nelson nodded. He heard her light a cigarette as she dressed. When she had finished she ripped off his right eyepatch.

'There now, we're ready to go,' she said, ignoring Nelson's anguished yells.

'That's the wrong eye,' he said.

'Oh shit,' said his mother and ripped off the other one, turned it upside down and stuck it over his right eye. The smoke from the cigarette in her mouth trickled up into her eye and she held it half shut. Nelson could see the bright points of sweat shining through her make-up. She still hadn't got her breath back fully yet. She smelt of drink.

On the way out, the fat man with the rolled-up sleeves held out two fivers and Nelson's mother put them into her purse.

'The boy – never again,' he said, looking down at Nelson.

They took the Number Twelve to St John the Baptist's. It was the worst possible time because, just as they were going in, the bell rang for the end of a period and suddenly the quad was full of pupils, all looking at Nelson and his mother. Some sixth-year boys wolf-whistled after her and others stopped to stare. Nelson felt a flush of pride that she was causing a stir. She was dressed in black satiny jeans, very tight, and her pink blouse was knotted, leaving her tanned midriff bare. They went into the office and a secretary came to the window.

'Yes?' she said, looking Mrs Skelly up and down.

'I'd like to see the Head,' she said.

'I'm afraid he's at a meeting. What is it about?'

'About him.' She waved her thumb over her shoulder at Nelson.

'What year is he?'

'What year are you, son?' His mother turned to him.

'First.'

'First Year. Oh, then you'd best see Mr MacDermot, the First Year Housemaster.' The secretary directed them to Mr MacDermot's office. It was at the other side of the school and they had to walk what seemed miles of corridors before they found it. Mrs Skelly's stiletto heels clicked along the tiles.

'It's a wonder you don't get lost in here, son,' she said as she knocked on the Housemaster's door. Mr MacDermot opened it and invited them in. Nelson could see that he too was looking at her, his eyes wide and his face smiley.

'What can I do for you?' he said when they were seated.

'It's him,' said Mrs Skelly. 'He's been skiving again. I caught him this morning.'

'I see,' said Mr MacDermot. He was very young to be a Housemaster. He had a black moustache which he began to stroke with the back of his hand. He paused for a long time. Then he said,

'Remind me of your name, son.'

' – Oh, I'm sorry,' said Mrs Skelly. 'My name is Skelly and this is my boy Nelson.'

'Ah, yes, Skelly.' The Housemaster got up and produced a yellow file from the filing cabinet. 'You must forgive me, but we haven't seen a great deal of Nelson lately.'

'Do you mind if I smoke?' asked Mrs Skelly.

'Not at all,' said the Housemaster, getting up to open the window.

'The trouble is, that the last time we were at that Sub-Attendance Committee thing they said they would take court action if it happened again. And it has.'

'Well, it may not come to that with the Attendance Sub-Committee. If we nip it in the bud. If Nelson makes an effort, isn't that right, Nelson?' Nelson sat silent.

'Speak when the master's speaking to you,' yelled Mrs Skelly.

'Yes,' said Nelson, making it barely audible.

'You're Irish too,' said Mrs Skelly to the Housemaster, smiling.

'That's right,' said Mr MacDermot. 'I thought your accent was familiar. Where do you come from?'

'My family come from just outside Derry. And you?'

'Oh, that's funny. I'm just across the border from you. Donegal.' As they talked, Nelson stared out the window. He had never heard his mother so polite. He could just see a corner of the playing fields and a class coming out with the Gym teacher. Nelson hated Gym more than anything. It was crap. He loathed the changing rooms, the getting stripped in front of others, the stupidity he felt when he missed the ball. The smoke from his mother's cigarette went in an arc towards the open window. Distantly he could hear the class shouting as they started a game of football.

'Nelson! Isn't that right?' said Mr MacDermot loudly.

'What?'

'That even when you are here you don't work hard enough.'

'Hmmm,' said Nelson.

'You don't have to tell me,' said his mother. 'It's not just his eye that's lazy. If you ask me the whole bloody lot of him is. I've never seen him washing a dish in his life and he leaves everything at his backside.'

'Yes,' said the Housemaster. Again he stroked his moustache. 'What is required from Nelson is a change of attitude. Attitude, Nelson. You understand a word like attitude?'

'Yes.'

'He's just not interested in school, Mrs Skelly.'

'I've no room to talk, of course. I had to leave at fifteen,' she said, rolling her eyes in Nelson's direction. 'You know what I mean? Otherwise I might have stayed on and got my exams.'

'I see,' said Mr MacDermot. 'Can we look forward to a change in attitude, Nelson?'

'Hm-hm.'

'Have you no friends in school?' asked the Housemaster.

'Naw.'

'And no interest. You see, you can't be interested in any subject unless you do some work at it. Work pays dividends with interest . . . ' he paused and looked at Mrs Skelly. She was inhaling her cigarette. He went on, 'Have you considered the possibility that Nelson may be suffering from school phobia?'

Mrs Skelly looked at him. 'Phobia, my arse,' she said. 'He just doesn't like school.'

'I see. Does he do any work at home then?'

'Not since he had his bag with all his books in it stolen.'

'Stolen?'

Nelson leaned forward in his chair and said loudly and clearly, 'I'm going to try to be better from now on. I am. I am going to try, sir.'

'That's more like it,' said the Housemaster, also edging forward.

'I am not going to skive. I am going to try. Sir, I'm going to do my best.'

'Good boy. I think, Mrs Skelly, if I have a word with the right people and convey to them what we have spoken about, I think there will be no court action. Leave it with me, will you? And I'll see what I can do. Of course it all depends on Nelson. If he is as good as his word. One more truancy and I'll be forced to report it. And he must realise that he has three full years of school to do before he leaves us. You must be aware of my position in this matter. You understand what I'm saying, Nelson?'

'Ah ken,' he said. 'I know.'

'You go off to your class now. I have some more things to say to your mother.'

Nelson rose to his feet and shuffled towards the door. He stopped.

'Where do I go, sir?'

'Have you not got your timetable?'

'No sir. Lost it.'

The Housemaster, tut-tutting, dipped into another file, read a card and told him that he should be at R.K. in Room 72. As he left, Nelson noticed that his mother had put her knee up against the Housemaster's desk and was swaying back in her chair, as she took out another cigarette.

"Bye, love,' she said.

When he went into Room 72 there was a noise of oos and ahhs from the others in the class. He said to the teacher that he had been seeing Mr MacDermot. She gave him a Bible and told him to sit down. He didn't know her name. He had her for English as well as R.K. She was always rabbiting on about poetry.

'You, boy, that just came in. For your benefit, we are talking and reading about organisation. Page 667. About how we should divide our lives up with work and prayer. How we should put each part of the day to use, and each part of the year. This is one of the most beautiful passages in the whole of the Bible. Listen to its rhythms as I read.' She lightly drummed her closed fist on the desk in front of her.

' "There is an appointed time for everything, and a time for every affair under the heavens. A time to be born and a time to die; a time to plant and a time to uproot . . ." '

'What page did you say, Miss?' asked Nelson.

'Six-six-seven,' she snapped and read on, her voice trembling, ' "A time to kill and a time to heal; a time to wear down and a time to build. A time to weep and a time to laugh; a time to mourn and a time to dance . . ." '

Nelson looked out of the window, at the tiny white H of the goal posts in the distance. He took his bubble-gum out and stuck it under the desk. The muscles of his jaw ached from chewing the now flavourless mass. He looked down at page 667 with its microscopic print, then put his face close to it. He tore off his eyepatch, thinking that if he was going to become blind then the sooner it happened the better.

My Dear Palestrina

'**C**OME ON, LOVE, it's for your own good,' she said.
Rooks from the trees above set up a slow, raucous
cawing. Cinders had spilled on the footpath and they
cracked and spat beneath their shoes, echoing in the arch of
the trees overhead, as they walked the mile from the town to
Miss Schwartz's place. The boy stayed one pace behind and
slightly to the left of his mother. To show her determination,
she had begun by taking his hand but it seemed foolish to be
seen dragging a boy of his age. Although now they were
separate they were so far gone along the road that she knew
she had won. The boy stopped at the old forge and stared at
the door into the dark, listening to the high pinging of the
blacksmith's hammer.

'Don't have me to go back, Danny, or I'll make an example
of you.' She waited, looking over her shoulder at him. His
eyes were still red from crying.

Miss Schwartz had a beautifully polished brass knocker on
her black front door. It resounded deep within the house. It
seemed a long time before she answered. When she did, it
was with politeness.

'Yes, can I help you?'

The boy's mother smiled back and nodded down the path
to where the boy was standing.

'I want him to have piana lessons,' she said.

31

Mrs McErlane, panting after the walk, fell into an arm-chair, propped her bag on her knee and listened as Miss Schwartz struck single notes for her Danny to sing. His voice was clear but not rich and still had reverberations of the long afternoon's crying in it. Her long pale finger poked about the piano and no matter where it went Danny's voice followed it. Then she played clusters of notes and Danny repeated them. She asked the boy to turn away and struck a note.

'Can you find that note?' and Danny played it. She did this again and again and each time the boy found it. At the doorstep on the way out Miss Schwartz said that the pleasure in teaching would be hers. *Auf wiedersehen*.

'Did you hear that?' said Mrs McErlane on the way home. 'Anyway it will be good for you. It's a lovely thing to have. The others is too old to learn now.'

Danny said nothing but hunched his shoulders against the darkness and the cold of the night that was coming on.

'I hated to think of that piana going to waste,' she said.

Because the McErlanes had a boy young enough to learn, it was they who got the piano when Uncle George died. They also got a lawn mower and a vacuum cleaner, even though they had no carpet in the house.

The piano came in the night when Danny was in bed. When he had visited Uncle George, Danny would slip into the front room on his own and climb up on the piano stool and single-finger notes. He liked to play the white ones because afterwards, when he struck a black note it was so sad that it gave him a funny feeling in his tummy. The piano stool had a padded seat which opened. Inside were wads of old sheet music with film stars' pictures on the front.

Bing Crosby, Johnny Ray, Rosemary Clooney. He had heard her singing on the radio.

A cannon-ball don't pay no mind
Whether you're gentle or you're kind.

32

It was about a civil war. He liked the way she twirled her voice. When he tried to sing that song he always put on an American accent.

> Two brothers on their way
> One wore blue and one wore grey.

After school he walked to his first lesson on a road that fumed with dry snow and wind. The door of the forge was closed and the place silent. On the way out a car passed him, returning to town. A white face pressed itself up against the back window. White hair, blue glasses and a red tongue sticking out at him. Mingo. Danny hated Mingo, with his strange eyes and white fleshy skin. Some of the boys in school had told him that Mingo was from Albania and they were all like that there.

Miss Schwartz had a warm fire blazing in her front room.

'You must be cold,' she said. 'Come, warm your hands.'

Danny held out his chapped hands and felt the heat on them. He rubbed the warmed palms on his bare knees, trying to thaw them out. Miss Schwartz smiled.

'You are such a good-looking boy,' she said. Danny stood embarrassed, his brown eyes averted, looking down at the fire. His blond hair had been cuffed and ruffled by the wind and gave him a wild look.

'You look like the Angel Gabriel,' she said and pulled her mouth into a wide smile. 'Sit down — near the fire — and let me tell you about music.' She spoke with a strange accent, as if some of her words were squeezed into the wrong shape. Her mouth was elastic. Danny knew every word she said but it was not the way he had heard anybody talk before.

'What kind of music do you like?'

'I dunno,' said Danny after a moment's thought.

'Do you have a favourite singer?'

'I like Elvis.'

'Rubbish,' she said, still smiling. 'What I am going to tell you now you will not believe. You will not understand it, but I have to tell you all the same. I will teach you about things. I hope I will nurture in you a love you will never forget.' The smile had disappeared from her face and her eyes widened and drilled into Danny's. 'Music is the most beautiful thing in the world. Today beautiful is a word that has been dirtied, but I mean it truly. Beautiful.' She let the word hang in the air between them.

'Music is why I do not die. Other people – they have blood put in their arms,' she stabbed a fingernail at the inside of her elbow, 'I am kept alive by music. It is the food of love, as you say. I stress that you will not believe me, but what you *must* do is *trust* me. I will show it to you if you will let me. Rilke says that music begins where speech ends – and he should know.'

Danny looked at her and the two pin-head reflections of the fire in her eyes. She was good-looking, with a long thin face and a broad mouth which she was constantly contorting as she wrestled to make the strange words clear. She did not wear lipstick like his mother. Her jet black hair was pulled back into a knot at the back of her neck and her parting was straight, as if ruled. Danny had seen her from the back when she played the organ in church and occasionally when she had come into the town shops, a dark figure hardly worth notice, her basket on her stiff forearm, her wrist to the sky. But here she seemed to fill the room with her talk and her flashing hands. All the time she sat on the edge of her chair, leaning towards him, talking into him. He swayed back as far as his stool would let him.

'Wait,' she said. She got up and went over to a bureau and took out a sheet of paper from a typewriter. She held it up.

'Look. Look hard at this.'

Danny looked but could see nothing, only the slight curl at the bottom of the page where it had lain in the machine.

'I give you a white sheet of paper. It is nothing. But the black marks . . . The black marks, Danny. That is what makes it important. The music, the words. They are the black marks,' she said, and her whole face blazed with passion. 'I am going to teach you those marks. Then I am going to teach you to make the most wonderful music from them. Come, let us begin.' As she sat down at the piano she snorted, 'Elvis Presley!'

When the lesson was over Miss Schwartz got up and went out, saying that they both deserved a cup of tea. Danny sat on the piano stool and looked at the room. It was a strange place, covered in pictures. Behind the pictures the wallpaper was dark brown, or else so old that it looked dark brown. There were plants in pots standing in saucers all over the place. Large dark green spikes with leathery leaves, small hanging plants, one with a pale flower on it. The wind pressured round the house and buffeted in the chimney. He could hear the ticking of fresh snow on the windows and the drone of a lorry taking the hill.

'I hope it lies,' he said to himself. The fire hissed and blew out a small feather of flame.

Miss Schwartz, carrying a tray, closed the door with her toe, which peeped out from her dressing-gown. It was of black silk, long to the floor and hanging loosely about her body. On the back it had a strange Chinese pattern in scarlet and green and silver threads. It reminded Danny of the one the magician wore in the Rupert Bear strip in the *Daily Express*.

'Now, while we drink our tea I will have to play you some music,' she said. She lifted the lid of one of the pieces of furniture and put on a record. She turned it up so loud that the music bulged in the room. Danny had never heard anything like it and he hated it. It had no tune and he kept waiting for somebody to sing but nobody did. He ate two biscuits and drank his tea as quickly as he could. Then she let him go.

35

On his way home the January wind cut his face and riffled the practice music he carried clenched under his arm. In the telephone wires above he heard the sounds of a peeled privet switch being whipped through the air again and again and again. At the forge he crossed the road to have a closer look. It was more of a shack than a building, with walls made of corrugated iron and hardboard of different faded and peeling colours. Someone had cleaned a paintbrush by the door or had tried out various colours on the wall. The place was surrounded by bits of broken and rusting machinery from farms. From the dark came the rhythmic sound of hammering. Danny edged into the open doorway and it stopped. A man's voice came out of the blackness.

'What do you want, lad?'

Danny jumped.

'C'mere,' said the voice. Danny moved to the threshold, trying to see into the gloom. 'What can I do for you?'

'Just looking.'

'Well, you'll never see from out there. Come in.'

The place smelt of metal and coke fumes and oil. Danny could make out a man in a leather apron. He looked too young to be a blacksmith, with his tight black curly hair.

'What's your name?' he asked. When Danny told him he thought for a moment. 'Your Da's a bus driver? Am I right or am I wrong?'

The man talked as he worked, heating a strip of metal in the coke of his fire and hammering it while it was red. Each hammer blow pulsed through Danny's head like the record at Miss Schwartz's.

'And what has you up this end of town?' Danny told him he was going to music.

'To Miss Warts and all?' he shouted. 'I wonder would she like this song?' He began to sing loudly, and bang his hammer to the rhythm, 'If I was a blackbird'. When he came to the line 'And I'd bury my head on her lily white breast', he

36

winked at Danny. He had a good voice and could get twirls into it — like Rosemary Clooney. When he had finished the song, he asked Danny about school. He didn't seem to think much of it because he said it was the worst place to learn anything. He talked a lot and Danny helped him to work the bellows for his fire. When he took the red hot metal out of the fire, it had tiny lights that flashed and disappeared. The man said that that was the dust touching it and burning up. As the smith worked, Danny looked at his arms, not muscled, but tight with sinews and strings, pounding at the metal. He shouted to make himself heard over his work.

'The schools make the people they want. They get rid of their cutting edge. That's how they keep us quiet.' He nodded that he wanted Danny to pump harder. 'It'll not always be like that. Our time will come, boy, and it'll not be horseshoes we'll be beating out. No, sir.'

Danny was breathless with the pumping. The blacksmith looked at him, raising one eyebrow.

'Are you the lad that was very ill not so long ago?'

Danny breathed and nodded.

'Then maybe you better quit and be off home.'

Danny picked up his music from the cluttered bench and blew the brown rust from it. As he left the man shouted after him,

'Just give us a call any time you're passing, son.'

Danny tried to walk the road in step to the fading ring of his hammer.

When he came through the back door his mother yelled at him,

'Where's the good cap I knitted for you?'

'Oh, sorry, I left it behind.'

She began to help him unbutton his coat, scolding with concern.

'You are not strong yet, you know. I don't know what that

37

woman was thinking of, letting you out without it. Are your ears not freezing?'

'I'm O.K.'

'You are not indeed. I never met your equal for catching things. There's not much the doctors don't know about that you haven't had. Twice over maybe. You must look after yourself, Danny.'

The boy went up to his room and lay on the bed. His mother was right. He seemed to be constantly ill. The last time had been the worst. The one nice thing he could remember about it was having the bed made while he was in it. He would lie there while his mother pulled all the bed-clothes off, then she would straighten the sheet beneath him, tugging it with exaggerated grunts. 'The weight of you!' she would say. He would run his fingers fan-like across the smoothness under him. His mother, separating out the clothes and standing at the end of the bed, would flap the upper sheet to make it fall soothingly on top of him. It came slow and cool and milky down over him with a breath of cotton-smelling air. It was almost transparent and he could look down at his feet and see himself in a white world – his tent, his isolation. The light came through, but he was cut off. He made no attempt to take the sheet down from his face. He heard her voice, then felt the heavier blankets fall across his body, the light disappearing. Only then would he turn back the sheet and look at her. He had wanted to remain suspended in the moment of the sheet, in its relaxation and whiteness, but it always came to an end. He knew that he made peaks at his head and at his toes. He had seen furniture covered this way, and his grandfather in the hospital morgue.

'Now sit up for your medicine.' It had been white too. Cloying sweetness trying to disguise a revolting base flavour. His father gave him sixpence if he could keep it down. After a week he had a shilling on his bedside table. His mother opened *her* mouth when she gave him the stuff. She set the spoon down and lifted the bowl in readiness. His tongue furred with the mixture. Little squirts of warm saliva came into his mouth and he gagged but it stayed down. 'Good boy. Another sixpence. Sure, you'll be rich by the end of the bottle.'

Now he rolled off the bed and decided to go downstairs and let his mother hear what he had learned that day.

'First, empty that,' she said. Danny went to the compost heap at the bottom of the garden with the scraps. On the way back he swung the empty colander and listened to the quiet hoot and whine of the wind through its holes. He liked listening to things. In the room with the two clocks he liked to hear how the ticks would catch up with one another, have the same double tick for a moment and then whisper off into two separate ticks again. The hiss of Miss Schwartz's dressing-gown as she moved. The thin squeak of his compass as he opened its legs. The pop his father's lips made when he was lighting his pipe. He left the empty colander on the draining board.

'Are you ready?' he asked her. His mother listened to his scales, her head cocked to one side, drying her hands on her apron. He played them haltingly.

'There's not much of a tune to that,' she said. 'How much do you have to practise?'

'Until I get it right, she says.'

'Who's "she", something the cat brought in?'

'Miss Schwartz.'

'Have a bit of respect, Danny.'

Danny seemed to get it right with little effort, but what little he did he had to be goaded into by his mother. There was nothing Miss Schwartz taught him that he couldn't do after several attempts. So, in the first months, Miss Schwartz increased the level of difficulty and the duration of his practice pieces. And he was always able for them.

Along the sides of the lane that led to her house Danny saw the yellow celandine and the white ones with the strange smell. Wild garlic, she had called them. He met Mingo coming down the lane to where his father had parked the car. Mingo made a vulgar noise with his mouth as they passed but Danny ignored him. Miss Schwartz held the door open and he gave her the envelope with the clinking money in it.

Seated at the piano, he asked,

'Is Mingo any good?'

'Mingo?'

'The boy with the white hair that's just left.'

'Is that what you call him? That boy . . . ' she paused, 'is average.'

'Is he as good as me?'

'Do not worry about other people. You will go forward as fast as you are able.' She smiled at him the way he looked at her, then added, 'You knew more on your first day than Mingo, as you call him, will in all his life. Now let me hear you play.'

Danny played his piece and when he had finished she shrugged and smiled.

'It is perfect,' she said, 'but still it is mechanical. Danny, you are a little machine. A pianola. Listen.' She sat on the stool and began to play. Danny listened, watching her closed eyes, the almost imperceptible sway of her body as she stroked music from the notes. 'At this point it must sing. *Cantabile.*' She talked over her playing, pointing out to him where he had gone wrong. 'Now try it again.'

Danny played the piece again and when it was over Miss Schwartz's eyes sparkled.

'That was much better,' she said. 'Beautiful. You learn so quickly.'

'I can't play like that at home,' he said, 'but here it's different.'

'I think,' said Miss Schwartz, 'it is time for an examination. It will please your mother. And I think it will please you because we will get a trip to the city. And . . . ' she added after more thought, 'it will please me. I will write a note to your mother. Although I will not say this in the letter, if you have any difficulties with the bus fare I will pay it myself. Do not say it, of course, if there are no difficulties.'

They began to work on a new piece by her darling Schubert and when she felt they had accomplished enough she got up and made tea.

Alone in the room, Danny stared at the pictures. Silhouettes, she called them. Jet black outlines of composers she had named. Beethoven, Mahler on the tips of his toes, Schubert. He liked Beethoven the best, the way his hair sprouted in all directions.

As they drank their tea she played again the record that she had played at their first lesson. Now Danny knew it and could hum the melody as it played.

Some weeks ago, when she had come back in with the tea, she had found Danny in the corner, crouched looking at her records. She kept them in a huge set of books, each page with a circular hole in it so that you could see the label of the record. Danny turned the stiff pages of the records, carefully looking at the labels, scarlet ones with a dog barking into a horn, green ones with the title in tilted writing. He took out a record and looked closely at its surface, angling it to the light. Intense black with light shining in the grooves. She handled them like eggs. When she came in all she said was, 'Be careful, Danny.' She poured the tea and then continued her sentence, 'or they will end up like this.' She leaned over and lifted a record which had a large bite out of its side.

'Some boys who come here are not as careful as you. Goodbye, Dinu Lipatti. I think I will have to make a flowerpot out of you. You see?' She pointed to one of her plants. A record had been folded up in some way to make a container. 'You heat it and you mould it until it is the shape you want. I

41

hate to waste anything. That's what comes of the war.' She bit into her gingersnap and said through her chewing,

'I would like to stand on his glasses.'

Danny liked to dip his into his tea and bite the warm, mushy sweetness.

When he handed Miss Schwartz's note to his mother, she ruffled his hair with her hand.

'You're losing your blondness,' she said, 'but the sun in the summer should bring it back again.' When she had finished the letter, the boy looked at her for a decision.

'Yes, you can go,' she said. 'But you'll have to stay the night. I'll not have you travelling that much in one day. Maybe your Aunt Letty would keep you.'

In the city they went to the Assembly Rooms and Danny passed his examination with the highest commendation. On the way down the steps, Miss Schwartz took his hand and although he made a slight attempt to take it away, she held tightly on to it. Then without looking at him, staring straight ahead into the rush hour traffic, she said,

'It's *not* too late. You can be great. If you try you can be really great.' She squeezed his hand so hard it hurt. Then she let it go.

'Did you say that to me?' asked Danny.

'Yes, Danny. To you.'

Afterwards they met a friend of Miss Schwartz's and went for tea in The Cottar's Kitchen. Danny had never seen her in such a joyful mood. She laughed and talked and praised him so much that he became embarrassed. She called him *'mein Lieber'* and introduced him to her friend as her star pupil, her *Wunderkind*.

'. . . and this is Mr Wyroslaski. He plays the cello in a symphony orchestra.'

He was a tall man with a very thin face. He had dark brown

eyes, deep eyes, not unlike Miss Schwartz's own. His hair was very long, almost like a woman's.

'Why do all music people have funny names?' Danny asked.

'Like what?' asked Miss Schwartz.

'Like Schwartz and Wyro . . . Wyro — your name,' he said, nodding at her friend, 'and all those composers.'

'Names do not matter; you, *mein Lieber*, will be a great musician one day.'

'My name is Danny McErlane,' and the way he said it made them all laugh. Miss Schwartz leaned across the table and smacked a kiss off Danny's forehead. He blushed and looked down at his plate.

'Besides,' said Mr Wyroslaski, 'there is John Field. He is an Irish composer. Names do not matter. What matters is the heart, the mind. Did you ever hear of a composer called Joe Green?'

Danny nodded that he hadn't.

'That is English for Giuseppe Verdi.'

'Who's he?' asked Danny. He joined uncertainly in the laughter his question had started. Mr Wyroslaski looked at him and produced a large handkerchief from his pocket. He slowly folded it into a pad which he licked and leaned over to Danny.

'Marysia, you leave your mark on everyone.' He rubbed Danny's forehead hard. It surprised Danny that Miss Schwartz had a first name. He sounded it over in his mind, Maur-ish-a, Maur-ish-a. He never imagined himself calling her anything but Miss Schwartz.

Today she looked different. When she had come out of the Ladies' Room her black hair was down, falling over her shoulders. Her normally sallow cheekbones were pink and her eyes seemed to sparkle and flash more than they did in the darkness of her sitting room at home. She wore a brown suit and a blouse of creamy lace. At her throat was a cameo brooch which matched the brown of her suit. It was the first time Danny had seen her legs, the first time he had seen her out of her dressing-gown.

Danny had begun to dislike Mr Wyroslaski. He had pulled away from the handkerchief but the man's bony hand had held the back of his neck so that he couldn't. Now as Wyroslaski listened to Miss Schwartz his mouth hung open and his eyebrows were raised like pause markings, as if he did not believe what she was saying. His face was prepared for laughter even though nothing funny was being said. They were talking too much. Danny began reading the stained menu. Then Wyroslaski lowered one eyebrow and said something in a foreign language at which Miss Schwartz laughed, covering her lower face with both hands. She replied to him in the same sort of language. Danny turned the menu over but there was nothing on the back of it.

Eventually she turned to Danny and said,

'He is such a handsome boy, my archangel, isn't he? *Mein Lieber*, we all must go. Your Aunt Letty will be worried about you. Mr Wyroslaski has kindly said that he will drive you there in his car. What do you say?'

'Thank you,' said Danny.

'We'll drop you off and I'll see you in good time for the bus in the morning.'

As they rose from the table, Mr Wyroslaski flicked his hair out from his collar with his knuckled cellist's hand.

The next day on the long bus journey home, Miss Schwartz was quiet and often seemed not to be interested in or understand what Danny said to her. She did point out the freshness and greenness of everything. Hedges flashed by, fields moved, mountains turned in the distance.

'It is spring. The sap is rising, quickening in all things. Do you not feel it?'

'No,' said Danny. And they lapsed into silence again.

At the next lesson, Miss Schwartz opened the door in her familiar black dressing-gown.

'Well, Danny, have you forgiven me?'

'What for?'

'I thought you had fallen out with me. Is that not so?'

'No.'

'You did not feel neglected?'

Danny began searching through his pages for his piece. He shrugged.

'It was *your* day, Danny. It was wrong of me to enjoy it.'
He set his music on the piano.

'What did you think of Mr Wyroslaski? Wasn't he . . . '

'He smiled too much,' Danny interrupted her.

'You *are* annoyed, aren't you, Danny?'

'No.'

And she touched his hair with her extended hand and her face opened in a warm smile of disbelief and delight.

After he played for her she asked,

'How did your mother like your certificate?'

'She says she's going to get Dad to frame it.'

'Tell her not to bother. There will be more. Bigger and better ones. And what's more, you can tell her I will give you extra lessons and it doesn't matter whether she can pay or not. Two a week for the price of one. How would you like that?'

Danny was not so sure, but he said yes to please her.

In July Danny's sister married. The remainder of the guests from the hotel all crowded into the McErlanes' front room after the reception. Danny's mother sat stunned and a little drunk. Her husband, Harry, was even more drunk, but had through practice learned to keep going. He was asking everybody what they would have to drink. Aunt Letty, who didn't drink, was helping him pour the whiskeys and uncork the stout. Danny sat in the corner with an orange juice in his hand which he dared not drink. Everybody that day had bought him an orange juice.

'Well, that's that,' said Harry, falling back into an armchair, his knees still bent. He waved his thumb in the direction of the corner. 'There's only one left. The shakings of the bag has yet to go.'

'It'll be a while yet, Harry,' said a neighbour, 'and he'll only go when the notion takes him. He'll not be forced.'

Harry blinked his eyes and focused on whoever had spoken. It was Red Tam.

'Tam, I hope you're not meaning anything by that remark.'

'What do you mean "meaning"?'

'About being forced. There was no forcing at today's match and well you know it.'

'The child, Harry,' warned Mrs McErlane.

'My girl is a good girl. She'd have none of that sort of filth.' Danny's father spat the last word out.

'Aye, I know. Time will tell,' said Red Tam.

'What the bloody hell do you mean, "time will tell"? If it's a fight you want, Red Tam, we'll settle it right now.' He struggled to escape from the armchair. Red Tam put up his hands and laughed.

'I'm saying, Harry, that time will prove you right. That's all. You're too jumpy, man.'

Harry was not so sure. Mrs McErlane interrupted.

'Danny is going to play the piano for us. Won't you, son? A bit of entertainment will settle us all.'

'The old Joanna,' someone shouted above the din.

'Good stuff.' A spatter of applause went round the room. Danny blushed.

'I'd wash my hands of any girl that would allow herself to be led into that sort of dirt before marriage.'

'It happens, Harry. It happens.'

'Not in my house it doesn't.'

'Look at big Maureen from Bank Street. Thirty-two years old, they say. At her age you'd think she'd have known better.'

'An animal,' said Harry, 'if ever there was one. There was that many of them she didn't know who to blame. The beasts of the field . . .'

'Stop it, Harry. The child,' hissed Mrs McErlane. 'Go and get your music, son.' She turned in explanation to her neighbour, saying, 'He's not allowed to play without it.'

Danny lurched shyly from the corner, saying that he wouldn't, but hands grabbed him and guided him through the crowded room to the piano. He took out the music for the piece he had just been practising.

'What are you going to give us?'

Danny propped the music up, opened the lid and the room became silent, except for the noise of somebody in the kitchen washing dishes. He began to play a movement from a Haydn sonata.

'That's grand stuff,' said his father proudly through the music.

'Very highfalutin' but good. It's well done,' said Red Tam.

'He has the touch,' said Mrs McErlane. 'So his music teacher tells me. Miss Schwartz, y'know. But you'd know to listen to him yourself.'

Danny played on, the glittering phrases mounting in elegance. Letty leaned in from the kitchen and, aware that she had to be quiet, hissed,

'Harry, will you have another stout?'

'I will, aye.'

'Whisht till we hear,' said Danny's mother. Red Tam rang notes on his empty whiskey glass with a horny fingernail and waved it at Letty. The piece came to an end and Danny's fingers had barely left the keys but they were folding away his music. Everyone applauded loudly.

'What was that?' asked Red Tam.

'Haydn,' said Danny his voice barely audible.

'Grand. Do you know any Winifred Atwell tunes? Now there *is* a pianist. How she does it I just do not know. The woman must have ten fingers on each hand. Do you know "The Black and White Rag" at all?' Red Tam took a gulp of his new whiskey. 'Did you ever hear any of her, Harry?'

'Aye, she's on the wireless, isn't she?'

'You can say that again. She's never off it. The money that woman must be making.' He shook his head in disbelief. 'And her coloured, too.'

'Do you like the rock and roll, Tam?' said Mrs McErlane, winking, 'I thought it would be right up your street.'

'Indeed I do not.'

'You're right there,' Danny's father joined in, 'I can't take this classic stuff the boy is at all the time but I know for sure the rock and roll is rubbish.'

'I like *some* classic stuff,' said Tam 'Mantovani . . . '

'I like good music — something with a bit of a tune to it,' Harry went on, 'Bing's my man.' He stuck the pipe in the corner of his mouth, his eyes closed, and he began to croon, slurring the words in an American accent,

'A'm dream — ing of a wha — ite Christmas.'

'Aye,' said Tam, interrupting the song, 'that's where the money is at. This rock and roll will not last.'

'It'll not be heard of in another year's time,' agreed Harry. 'The boy there could be making money before long. There's many's the dance band would snap him up if he was older. The classical stuff is all right. It gets the hands going. Good practice, y'know. But the bands is the place where the money is.'

'Or on the wireless,' added Tam. Harry rose and stood expansive and swaying in front of the fire.

'You did well at the speaking, Harry, for one that's not used to it,' said his wife.

48

'Aye. At least I kept it clean. Which is more than I can say for some.'

'Uncle Bob. Wasn't that a disgrace.'

One of the others, drunker than the rest, overheard and mimicked,

' "The bride and groom have just gone upstairs to get their things together." ' Half the people laughed again at the joke. Harry said,

'That man Bob has a mind like a sewer.'

Danny threaded his way to the door and once upstairs threw what was left of his orange down the lavatory.

They worked hard all though that summer, the boy in shirtsleeves at the piano, Miss Schwartz, despite the heat, still in her silk dressing-gown. One day Danny discovered that she wore nothing beneath it because when she bent over to point out some complexity in the score the overlap of her gown rumpled and he saw cradled there the white pear shape of one of her breasts. He pretended not to understand the notation but when she bent over again her dressing-gown was in order.

'The black marks, Danny. Pay attention to the black marks.'

He felt his knees shaky and could not concentrate to play any more.

After the lesson they would go out to the small garden and have tea beneath the apple tree, tea with no milk but a slice of lemon in it — a thing Danny had never heard of. Miss Schwartz had pointed out to him when the flowers had fallen off the tree and each week they inspected the swelling fruit. Lying back in striped deck chairs they both watched the flickering blue of the sky as it dodged between the leaves.

Miss Schwartz had resurrected from the attic an ancient wind-up gramophone on which she played records outdoors.

Danny came to know many pieces. Sometimes if there was a concert on the wireless she would open the kitchen window, turn the volume up full and point the set towards the garden. One day, during a performance of Mahler's '*Kindertotenlieder*', she said,

'You know, Danny, the reason I bought this house was because of the garden. We had one just like it when I was a girl. I was about your age when we had to leave it.'

'Where was it?'

'In Poland. A place called Praszka. I remember it as beautiful.'

'Why don't you go back?'

She laughed. 'Because I am too long away. The longer you are away the more you want to go back. And yet you realise the longer you are away the more impossible it is to return. The early monks had a phrase for it – what you suffer. If you died for God, that was simple. That was red martyrdom. If you left your country for God and lived in isolation, that was white martyrdom. To be an exile, to be cut off from your country is a terrible thing.' She smiled. 'I left, not for God, but for convenience. It was a time of fear.' She shuddered and looked up into the apple tree.

Danny sat stripped except for his shorts. He glanced up to where the music was coming from and saw himself reflected brightly in the window. His hair had grown longer and darker. Light from a spoon on the tray lying on the grass reflected into his face.

'But it is not so bad. There are compensations,' she said, smiling at him.

Many times on his way home Danny would stop off at the forge, if it was open, and listen to the blacksmith. He loved the way the man did not shave often and had black bristles on his chin like the baddies in cowboy comics. He was always joking and talking. 'Am I right or am I wrong?' was his

50

favourite phrase. One day, sitting astride his anvil, he talked about Miss Schwartz.

'She's a rum bird, isn't she?'

Danny nodded.

'Why do you agree with me? The nod of the head is the first sign of a yes-man. Well, are you just a yes-man?'

'No,' said Danny and laughed.

'This bloody country is full of yes-men and the most of them's working class.' He dismounted from the anvil and began to rake the fire to life. 'Yes, your honour, no, your honour. Dukes and bloody linen lords squeezing us for everything we've got, setting one side against the other. Divide and conquer. It's an old ploy and the Fenians and Orangemen of this godforsaken country have fallen for it again.' He began to work the bellows himself and the centre of the fire reddened. Danny loved the colour of blue that the small flames took on when the fire was heating up. He could feel the warmth of the fire on the side of his face and his bare arm. The smith was now talking into the fire.

'But a change is coming, Danny Boy. We must be positive. Prepare the ground. Educate the people. Look to the future the way Connolly and Larkin did in 1913.'

He threw the poker down among the fire-irons with a clang and turned to Danny. His face changed and he smiled.

'You haven't a baldy notion what I'm talking about, have you?'

'No.'

'But am I right or am I wrong?'

'You're right,' was always Danny's answer.

It was about this time that Danny began to notice a change in Miss Schwartz. She became moody and did not smile or laugh as much as she used to. One day when he arrived early for his lesson, panting from running most of the mile, it was a long time before she opened the door. When she did she was thrusting a handkerchief up her sleeve and she had obviously been crying. Her eyes were heavy-lidded and red.

When she went in, she said, 'Get your breath back,' and began to water her plants from a small Japanese tea-pot, turning her back on him. She talked to the plants the way other people would talk to a pet. She said it encouraged them to grow.

'Lavish love and attention on growing things and they will not let you down.'

'What about your apple tree? Do you talk to it?'

'It hears music from the house.' She smiled weakly at her own answer.

'But I know houses . . .'

'Your piece, Danny. I want to hear it.'

Danny gave a small, knowing smile. Miss Schwartz half reclined on the sofa at the bay window, her feet gathered beneath her. She turned to face the light and waited. Danny set his music on the chair and began to play. It was the opening movement of the Beethoven C sharp minor Sonata. She disliked calling it, 'The Moonlight'. Danny looked round to see if she had noticed, but her eyes were closed. He played on, trying to feel the music as she would have felt it. Sunlight slanted into the room and Danny thought her face looked haggard. Some of her tight hair had come adrift and hung down by her throat.

When he finished Miss Schwartz opened her eyes and they were glassy with tears.

'How beautiful, Danny,' she said in a whisper.

'You didn't notice,' he said, his feet swinging on the stool.

'What?'

'I played it without the music.'

Miss Schwartz came to him.

'How utterly superb,' she said, taking his face in her hands. She put her arms around his head and gave him a tight squeeze of joy. Danny sensed the huge softness of her breasts against his cheek, enveloping his face, the faded scent of her, the goosefleshy wedge at her throat.

'Oh Danny, how superb.' This time she held him at arm's length, watching his blushes rise. Danny tried to dismiss it.

'I practised it —

                   all week end,' he said.

'Oh Danny,' Miss Schwartz let a gasp out of her. 'Say that again.'

'I prac —

                   -tised it all week end.'

'Danny, your voice is breaking.' She put one hand over her mouth, a look of disbelief in her eyes. She sat down at the piano and asked him to sing some of the notes she played. His voice was accurate but kept flicking an octave down. She sat at the piano, her fingers poised above the keyboard, touching it but not heavily enough to depress the keys. Her head was bowed.

'The purest thing in the world is the voice of a boy before it breaks,' she said, 'before he gets hair. Before he begins to think things — like that.' Her face looked the same way as when he played badly.

'But I hardly even notice it, Miss.'

'I do and that is sufficient,' she said. 'Today in the garden I will play you purity.'

The kitchen was full of a mute bustling as she made the tea. Danny carried the tray out, she the record. It was a boy soprano singing Latin. A blackbird from the ridge-tiles of the roof sang loud enough to drown certain passages. When the music was finished Danny said,

'My Mum says to tell you that I'm going to Grammar School.'

'You passed your Qualifying!' Danny nodded. 'Oh, I'm delighted. Which school?'

'Our Lady's High.'

'Hm.' She thought for a moment and then smiled. 'They don't have a music teacher as yet.'

Danny sat in the school yard eating his cheese piece, a bottle of milk in his hand. He saw Mingo coming across to him, his white hair weaving through the crowd. He had started the Grammar in September as well, but everybody knew that his father was paying for him.

'Hiya, piss face,' said Mingo. 'You still going out to that black bitch for music?' Danny looked at him but could not answer because the tacky cheese had stuck to the roof of his mouth.

'Sucker,' said Mingo. 'I don't have to go any more. Haw-haw-haw.' He spoke the laughter in words.

'Why not?'

'Because my old woman just stopped me. She was talking to Schwartzy in town and she came home and said, "That's it, no more music for you, my lad." Haw-haw-haw. McErlane the sucker still has to go.'

'It's O.K. She's not bad.'

'She has a good pair of tits on her,' said Mingo, groping the air before him. 'She likes you, McErlane. You're her pet. Does she ever let you feel her?' Danny looked at Mingo's flickering white eyelashes — he was constantly blinking behind his tinted glasses. He wanted to punch him in his foul mouth. Instead Danny said,

'I saw them one day.'

'Her tits?'

'Yeah.'

'What were they like?'

'Just ordinary.' Danny gestured with his hands.

'How did you see them?'

'She opened her dressing-gown one day and she wasn't wearing a . . . thingy.'

54

'Liar, I don't believe you.'

Danny shrugged and threw his crusts into the waste-basket.

'Were they nice bloopy ones?'

'Yeah.'

Danny sucked the bluish watery milk through a straw until it was finished. It made a hollow rattling sound at the bottom of the bottle. He asked Mingo,

'Are you going to music to anybody else?'

'There isn't anybody for miles, thank God.'

'I don't think I'd want to go to anybody else.'

'Aye, not if she shows you her tits, I don't blame you.'

There was a pause. Danny laced the used straw into a knot of angles.

'She shows them to more than you,' said Mingo.

'What do you mean?'

'She's a ride.'

'What's a ride?'

'Haw-haw-haw, he doesn't know.' Mingo folded up with mock laughter. 'She's going to have a baby.'

'So what?'

'So she's a ride.'

'How do you know?'

'My Mum says.'

'Your Mum's . . . a ride,' said Danny.

Mingo suddenly reached out and grabbed Danny by the ear, digging his nails into it shouting,

'Nobody says that about my Mum.'

Danny yelled out in pain and punched. He struck Mingo on the nose and dislodged his glasses. Mingo let go of Danny's ear and turned and ran, clutching his glasses to his chest, a trickle of blood on his white upper lip. He stopped at the far side of the playground and made a large 'up ya' sign with two fingers. It began at the ground and ended above his head. He kept doing it, jumping up and down to exaggerate the gesture. Danny turned away in disgust and slotted the empty milk bottle into the crate.

The road to Miss Schwartz's place was ankle-deep in brown scuffling leaves. The apples on the tree had become ripe and she had given Danny one. He bit into it and a section of its white flesh came away with a crack. Juice wet his chin.

'It must be the music,' he said crunching.

Now he practised with real determination, getting up with his father and doing an hour before school. He had to wait until his father went out because he said he couldn't stand the racket first thing in the morning. He did another hour in the evening before his father came in. His mother didn't seem to mind. She slept through the morning session and she would be out in the kitchen making Harry's dinner for most of the evening practice. She was glad to see the piano used so much. One evening Danny's mother came in to lay the table and stood watching him play.

'Your hair is getting darker. I thought the sun would have helped,' she said. Danny stopped playing.

'Mum,' he said, 'Miss Schwartz wants to know if you could pay her in advance for this term.'

'Oh, I don't think so. Look at the money I had to lay out for your uniform for the High.' She went to the cupboard and looked in the jar on the top shelf.

'No, tell her I'm sorry but I just can't do it.'

'A whole lot of her pupils are leaving.'

'Why's that?'

'I don't know,' said Danny, closing the lid of the piano.

It was shortly after this that the biscuits stopped. Miss Schwartz apologised and said that she was getting too fat. However, they still had tea together.

Danny's father, being a bus driver, got the pick of all the papers left in his bus, but the only one he would bring home was the *Daily Express*. He had a great admiration for it.

'First with everything,' he said, 'and no dirt.'

From his armchair he read a piece to Danny that said that the Russians had launched a satellite into space and that it would be possible to see it for the next few evenings if conditions were right.

'It's wonderful too,' he said nodding his head. 'At one end of the world the Russians is firing things into outer space and we still have a blacksmith in the town shoeing horses.'

'He says he knows you,' said Danny.

'Who?'

'The blacksmith.'

'When were you talking to him?' His father's voice had risen in pitch.

Danny shrugged.

'After music,' he said.

'Well, you'll just stop it. You hear me? If I catch you in that forge I'll take my belt off to you.'

The loud voice brought Danny's mother out from the kitchen. Her head was cocked to one side with curiosity and concern.

'Who's this?' she asked.

'You know who – the blacksmith. If he's pouring the same poison into your ear, son, as he's been spewing out in the pub, he's a bad influence. He'd have you into guns and God knows what. Denying religion at the top of his voice.'

'God forgive him,' said Mrs McErlane.

'Aye, and what's more he said they weren't serious in 1922 because they didn't shoot a single priest.'

'Did he say that?'

'Do you hear me, Danny, steer clear of vermin like that or you'll feel the weight of my hand.'

The next lesson Danny had he told Miss Schwartz of the satellite. She agreed that they should go out at six and try to see it.

The night was cold, black and clear as a diamond. A swirl of stars covered the sky so that it seemed impossible to put a finger between two of them. And they stood and waited, their necks craned.

'Isn't it marvellous,' Miss Schwartz said. Danny said nothing. His eye was searching for the satellite.

'Can you see it?' he asked.

When they stopped walking, the crackling underfoot ceased and the silence seemed enormous. In the frost nothing moved. Then Miss Schwartz whispered,

'Look. Look there.' It was as if she had seen an animal and to speak would frighten it.

'Where?'

'Follow my finger'

In the darkness Danny had to get close to look along the line of her arm. He smelt her perfume and the slightest taint of her own smell, felt his face brush the texture of her clothing.

'There,' she said, 'can you see it? Like a moving star. A little brighter than the rest.'

'Oh yes. I can see it now.'

They stood in silence, close to each other, watching the pin-point of light threading its way up the sky from the horizon. To their left was the faint orange dome of light from the town. When the satellite was directly above them it paused, or seemed to pause, and they held their breath, their faces dished to the sky. Miss Schwartz put her hand round Danny's shoulder.

'How utterly lonely,' she said. 'The immensity of it frightens me.'

They were silent for a long time, watching its descent down the other side of the sky, moving yet hardly moving. Some miles away a dog barked. A car's headlights fanned into the sky and they heard its engine as soft as breathing. Miss Schwartz said in a whisper,

'The music of the spheres. Do you hear it, Danny?'

'No. What is it?'

'It's a sort of silence,' she said and in the darkness he knew that she was smiling. Suddenly she returned to her normal voice.

'What I don't understand, Danny,' her fingers began to knead his shoulder, 'is how it stays up there. I'm very silly about these things. Why does it not fall down?'

'It's kind of suspended. Outside earth's gravity. I think the moon pulls it one way and the earth pulls the other and nobody wins — so it just stays up there. Something like that anyway. The papers say it will fall back to earth after a few months.'

'Caught between the heavens and the earth. How knowledgeable you are, Danny.'

'The science teacher told us today at school.' He began to tremble with the cold.

'Oh, but you are shivering. We must go in or your mother will be angry with me. If you catch a chill she will have my life.'

Inside Miss Schwartz made tea while Danny waited, sitting on his stool by the fire, listening to a record he had chosen himself.

'I'm glad that you picked that one,' she said when she came into the room. 'On Sunday at church I will play you your favourite.'

'Which?'

'The Bach. *"Liebster Jesu, wir sind hier"*.'

'What does that mean?'

' "Jesus we are here".'

'Seems a funny thing to say. You'd think he'd know that.'

'Sometimes I wonder,' she said, approaching her tea with her mouth because it was so hot without milk or a slice of lemon.

On his way home Danny followed the wobbling yellow disc his torch made on the ground. He was not afraid of the dark but felt protected by it in some way. He noticed from a distance that light was coming from the forge. The door was open and a slice of the roadway in front of it visible. The blacksmith must have heard him because when Danny stopped outside he began to sing 'Oh Danny Boy'.

'Come in,' he shouted. From the threshold Danny refused.

'Why not?'

'My Dad says I'm not allowed.'

The blacksmith laughed and said that he had a fair idea why.

'What would he do if he caught you here?'

'Take his belt off to me.'

The man snorted and came to Danny in the doorway. He rucked up his leather apron and thrust his hands into his pockets.

'Danny,' he said and there was a long pause. 'You're coming to an age now when you've got to think. Don't accept what people tell you — even your father. Especially your father. And that includes me.'

Danny eased his hip on to a large tractor tyre propped by the door.

'Your Dad and I have very different views of things. He accepts the mess the world is in whereas I don't. We've got to change it — by force if necessary.'

'Did you see the satellite?' asked Danny. The blacksmith nodded and laughed.

'It takes the Russians. I bet the Yanks feel sickened. That's an example of what I'm talking about. Equal shares and equal opportunity leads to progress, Danny. The classless society. It'll happen in Ireland before long. There's nothing surer. Am I right or am I wrong?'

Danny smiled and said that he would have to go. The blacksmith touched him on the shoulder.

'If you want to come back here, Danny, you come. The belt shouldn't stop you. You've got to be your own man, Danny Boy.'

'I'll maybe see you.'

On the road Danny waited for the hammer blows so that he could walk in step but none came and he had to choose his own rhythm.

On Sunday Danny waited to hear the familiar thumping sound of Miss Schwartz taking her place in the organ loft. She was not the same religion as the McErlanes but she had told Danny that she had needed the money and that it was a chance to play regularly on the best organ for a radius of twenty miles. After mass she had taken him up several times into the loft and he had been astonished by the sense of vibration, the wheezes and puffs and clanks of the machinery which he hadn't heard from the church. He loved the power of the instrument when she opened the stops fully to clear the church.

He heard the door of the organ loft close and was surprised when he looked round to see a man. He was bald with a horseshoe of white hair and horn-rimmed spectacles. Throughout the distribution of communion he played traditional hymns with a thumping left hand and a scatter of wrong notes. Afterwards he drove away in a white Morris Minor.

Outside on the driveway Father O'Neill talked to Danny's mother. The boy was sent on ahead while they talked. All that Sunday the house was full of whispers. Danny would come into a room and the conversation would stop. He thought Miss Schwartz must be ill.

The next day, the Monday before Christmas, when he came home from school his mother was sitting at the table writing a letter. He gathered his music and was about to go out when she called him.

'Here's a note for your music teacher.' Then she added, 'Don't be too disappointed, son.'

'What do you mean?'

'Never mind. Just you take that to your teacher and maybe she'll explain.'

On the road the wind was cold. Some hailstones had fallen and gathered into seams along the side of the road. The wind hurt the lobes of his ears and the tip of his nose.

He gave Miss Schwartz the note and she opened it jaggedly with a finger. She chinked the money into her hand, then read the letter. She looked as if she was going to cry but she stopped herself by biting her lip. Her teeth were nice and straight and white.

'Play for me,' she said.

Danny began to play the Field Nocturne he had been practising. The dark descended slowly. When he had finished she said,

'Let us not have a lesson. Let us play all the best things.'

'You didn't play the organ on Sunday. Were you sick?'

'Yes. I was indisposed.' She thought for a while, then put her hand to the back of her head and untied her hair. With a shake she let it fall darkly forward.

'I'm pregnant,' she said. Danny nodded.

'That means I'm going to have a baby.'

'Yes, I know.'

'They don't want me any more.'

'Why not? You're the best organist I've ever heard.'

'You can't have heard many. No more talk, Danny. That's enough. What are you going to play?'

'Can I have the light on?'

'No,' she said. 'Play me the Schubert. You know it well enough to play in the dark. It makes the other senses better. In the dark we are all ears, are we not?' Her voiced sounded wet, as if she had been crying.

'Which one?'

'The G flat.'

Danny began to play. Somehow he felt a sense of occasion, as if she was willing him to play better than he had ever played before. To feel, as she had so often urged him, the heart and soul of what Schubert had heard when he wrote down the music. In the dark he was aware of her slight swaying as he played. Now she sat forward on the sofa, her long hair hanging like curtains on each side of the pale patch of her face. She sat like a man, her knees wide apart, her elbows resting on them. The melody, more sombre than he had played it before, flowed out over the rippling left hand. Then came the heavy base like a dross, holding the piece to earth. The right hand moved easily into the melody again, the highest note seeming never to reach high enough, pinioned by a ceiling Schubert had set on it. Like the black notes he had struck in Uncle George's room by himself creating a disturbing ache. The piece reached its full development and swung into its lovely main melody for the last time. It ended quietly, dying into a hush. Both were silent, afraid to break the spell that had come with the music. Danny heard Miss Schwartz give a sigh, a long shuddering exhalation and he too sighed. She leaned forward and switched on a small orange lamp which stood on the side table.

'Danny, you are my last pupil. They have taken all the others away from me. But I do not care about them. They are money. But you are the best. You are more than that. You are the best thing I have ever had and when they try to take you away from me . . . ' She stopped and dipped her face into the handkerchief she had rolled in her hand. She looked up at him and began again.

'This is your last lesson. Your mother does not allow you to come here again.'

'Why not?' Danny's voice was high and angry. Miss Schwartz raised her shoulders and splayed out her hands.

'I think in our time together we have accomplished much,

Danny. There is so much more technique that you have to learn. But your heart must be right. Without it technique is useless. Sometimes I am ungenerous and doubt others' sensitivity. It is hard to believe that someone can feel as deeply as oneself. It is difficult not to think of oneself as the centre of the universe. But I believe in yours, Danny. I see it in your eyes, in your face. Do you know what a frisson is?'

'No.'

'It is a feeling that you get. Indescribable. A shivering. Your hair stands on end when you hear or read or know something that is exceptionally beautiful. Did you ever get that?'

'No.'

'Have you ever cried listening to a piece of music — not from sadness but from the sheer beauty of it? Have you ever *felt* like crying?'

'No. I don't think I have.' Danny wanted to please her but she asked the question with such a seriousness, beseeched him, that to tell a lie would have been wrong.

'I can only compare it to something which you have not yet experienced. Something you would not understand. But it will come. I'm sure it will come. That is what is wrong with this world. People are like the beasts of the field. They know nothing of music or tenderness. Anyone whom music has spoken to — really spoken to — must be gentle, must be kind — could not be guilty of a cruelty.'

She stood up and was walking back and forth with her fists tight.

'*Mein Lieber*, in the light the pale people see nothing. The glare blinds them. It is easy to hurt what you cannot see. To drop bombs a million miles away.' She stopped walking and pointed her finger straight at him. 'One of your Popes had a great thing to say once. He had been listening to some music by Palestrina with Palestrina himself. He said to him, "The law, my dear Palestrina, ought to employ your music to lead hardened criminals to repentance." Do you think this,' and she hissed out the s sound, 'this town would do this to me if they had truly heard one bar of Palestrina? Listen. Listen to this.'

She stamped across the room and took out one of the books of records. She put one on and turned the volume up full and announced,

'Palestrina.'

She sat down on the sofa, rigid with anger, electricity almost sparking from her hair.

'Close your eyes,' she commanded.

Danny closed his eyes and let his hands rest on his bare knees. The unaccompanied singing seemed to infuse the room with sanctity. The clear male voices, intricate and contrapuntal, became an abstraction. Stairs of sound ascending and yet descending at the same instant. Danny thought of what she had said, her tirade. He thought of being taken away from this room, never to be allowed back again to talk and work with Miss Schwartz. Never to be allowed to call in on the blacksmith and be talked to as if he were a man. The garden, the sunlight, the tea. Her concern for everything he did and said. The pumping of the bellows and smell of coke. Her perfume and her laugh, her plants, her music. Her bare breast. Am I right or am I wrong, *mein Lieber*? He thought of being deprived of all this, never to be allowed back to it. And he began silently in his own dark to cry.

Miss Schwartz saw the tears squeeze from his eyes and she jumped from the sofa, all her anger gone, and rushed to him. In her haste the tail of her dressing-gown caught a pot-plant and it tumbled to the floor. Black loam spilled out and the dislodged plant fell from the pot, displaying its tangled skirt of white roots. She knelt before him, her arms about his waist. She too was crying. She kissed his knees and he felt her long hair tickle his legs as she swung her head back and forth.

'You are one of us, my love.'

She continued to weep, the tears streaming down her face, wetting her chin. It was only now that Danny felt her fatness through her gown, not soft fatness, but a hard pumped-up bigness pressing against him. She held him so tightly, so closely that after a time he was unsure whether the hardness belonged to him or to her. To stop himself falling off the stool he put his hands around her neck and as she pressed her cheek to his he felt the sliding wetness of it. She smelled beautiful in the darkness of her hair. She began to move in time to the music, crushing his face to hers. He heard and felt her mouth implode small kisses on the side of his face, moving towards his mouth, but he wrenched his head to the side, not knowing what to do. They stayed like that until the record ended with a hiss and the tick-tick-tick of the over-run.

Miss Schwartz got up from her knees and straightened her dressing-gown. She pushed back her hair and sniffed loudly.

'Go, Danny. Now. At once.'

He stopped at the door, his hand on the handle. She was kneeling again, sweeping the springy black loam with her hands into a pile on the mat. She knelt on her gown so that it pulled taut over the hump of her stomach and for the first time Danny saw how big it was. Her hands, dirtied with the soil, hung useless from her wrists.

'Promise me one thing before you go,' she said. 'Find a good teacher. *Bitte, mein Lieber*. You might yet be great. Please – for me?'

Danny, unable to find the right words, nodded and left. Running in the swirling snow, the only thing he could think of was that she had not given him tea.

When he got home there was the worst row ever. Danny screamed and shouted at his mother, hardly knowing what he was saying. The answers they gave him he could not understand. They called her a slut and spoke of marriage and sin and Our Blessed Lady. He asked to be allowed back, he cried and pleaded, but his father ended it by thrashing him with his belt and threatening to take an axe to the piano.

Danny ran out into the night, down the garden, where he had built himself a hut of black tarred boards.

'Let him go, let him go,' he heard his mother scream.

The snow had lain and was thick under foot. The fields stretched white away from the white garden. Danny crawled into the darkness of his hut and squatted on the floor. He put his arms around his ankles and rested his wet cheek on his knees. He did not know how many hours it was he stayed like that.

He heard his mother coming out, her feet crunching and squeaking on the frozen snow.

'Danny,' she called, 'Danny.' She bowed down into the hut and took him by the arm. He had lost his will and when she drew him out, he came. The boy walked as if palsied, stiff and angular with the cold, his mother supporting him beneath his arm. He was numb, past the shivering point.

'Come into the heat, love,' she said, 'come in from the night. Join us.'

Life Drawing

AFTER DARKNESS FELL and he could no longer watch the landscape from the train window, Liam Diamond began reading his book. He had to take his feet off the seat opposite and make do with a less comfortable position to let a woman sit down. She was equine and fifty and he didn't give her a second glance. To take his mind off what was to come, he tried to concentrate. The book was a study of the Viennese painter Egon Schiele who, it seemed, had become so involved with his thirteen-year-old girl models that he ended up in jail. Augustus John came to mind: 'To paint someone you must first sleep with them', and he smiled. Schiele's portraits — mostly of himself — exploded off the page beside the text, distracting him. All sinew and gristle and distortion. There was something decadent about them, like Soutine's pictures of hanging sides of beef.

Occasionally he would look up to see if he knew where he was but saw only the darkness and himself reflected from it. The streetlights of small towns showed more and more snow on the roads the farther north he got. To stretch, he went to the toilet and noticed the faces as he passed between the seats. Like animals being transported. On his way back he saw a completely different set of faces, but he knew they looked the same. He hated train journeys, seeing so many people, so many houses. It made him realise he was part of things whether he liked it or not. Seeing so many unknown people through their back windows, standing outside shops, walking the streets, moronically waving from level crossings, they grew amorphous and repulsive. They were going about their static lives while he had a sense of being on the move. And yet he knew he was not. At some stage any one of those people might travel past his flat on a train and see him in the act of pulling his curtains. The thought depressed him so much that he could no longer read. He leaned his head against the window and although he had his eyes closed he did not sleep.

The snow, thawed to slush and refrozen quickly, crackled under his feet and made walking difficult. For a moment he was not sure which was the house. In the dark he had to remember it by number and shade his eyes against the yellow glare of the sodium street lights to make out the figures on the small terrace doors. He saw Fifty-six and walked three houses farther along. The heavy wrought-iron knocker echoed in the hallway as it had always done. He waited, looking up at the semicircular fan-light. Snow was beginning to fall, tiny flakes swirling in the corona of light. He was about to knock again or look to see if they had got a bell when he heard shuffling from the other side of the door. It opened a few inches and a white-haired old woman peered out. Her hair was held in place by a net a shade different from her own hair colour. It was one of the Miss Harts but for the life of him he couldn't remember which. She looked at him, not understanding.

'Yes?'

'I'm Liam,' he said.

'Oh, thanks be to goodness for that. We're glad you could come.'

Then she shouted over her shoulder, 'It's Liam.'

She shuffled backwards, opening the door and admitting him. Inside she tremulously shook his hand, then took his bag and set it on the ground. Like a servant, she took his coat and hung it on the hall stand. It was still in the same place and the hallway was still a dark electric yellow.

'Bertha's up with him now. You'll forgive us sending the telegram to the College but we thought you would like to know,' said Miss Hart. If Bertha was up the stairs then she must be Maisie.

'Yes, yes, you did the right thing,' said Liam. 'How is he?'

'Poorly. The doctor has just left – he had another call. He says he'll not last the night.'

'That's too bad.'

By now they were standing in the kitchen. The fireplace was black and empty. One bar of the dished electric fire took the chill off the room and no more.

'You must be tired,' said Miss Hart, 'it's such a journey. Would you like a cup of tea? I tell you what, just you go up now and I'll bring you your tea when it's ready. All right?'

'Yes, thank you.'

When he reached the head of the stairs she called after him, 'And send Bertha down.'

Bertha met him on the landing. She was small and withered and her head reached to his chest. When she saw him she started to cry and reached out her arms to him saying,

'Liam, poor Liam.'

She nuzzled against him, weeping. 'The poor old soul,' she kept repeating. Liam was embarrassed feeling the thin arms of this old woman he hardly knew about his hips.

'Maisie says you have to go down now,' he said, separating himself from her and patting her crooked back. He watched her go down the stairs, one tottering step at a time, gripping the banister, her rheumatic knuckles standing out like limpets.

He paused at the bedroom door and for some reason flexed his hands before he went in. He was shocked to see the state

71

his father was in. He was now almost completely bald except for some fluffy hair above his ears. His cheeks were sunken, his mouth hanging open. His head was back on the pillow so that the strings of his neck stood out.

'Hello, it's me, Liam,' he said when he was at the bed. The old man opened his eyes flickeringly. He tried to speak. Liam had to lean over but failed to decipher what was said. He reached out and lifted his father's hand in a kind of wrong handshake.

'Want anything?'

His father signalled by a slight movement of his thumb that he needed something. A drink? Liam poured some water and put the glass to the old man's lips. Arcs of scum had formed at the corners of his sagging mouth. Some of the water spilled on to the sheet. It remained for a while in droplets before sinking into dark circles.

'Was that what you wanted?' The old man shook his head. Liam looked around the room, trying to see what his father could want. It was exactly as he had remembered it. In twenty years he hadn't changed the wallpaper, yellow roses looping on an umber trellis. He lifted a straight-backed chair and drew it up close to the bed. He sat with his elbows on his knees, leaning forward.

'How do you feel?'

The old man made no response and the question echoed around and around the silence in Liam's head.

Maisie brought in tea on a tray, closing the door behind her with her elbow. Liam noticed that two red spots had come up on her cheeks. She spoke quickly in an embarrassed whisper, looking back and forth between the dying man and his son.

'We couldn't find where he kept the teapot so it's just a tea-bag in a cup. Is that all right? Will that be enough for you to eat? We sent out for a tin of ham, just in case. He had nothing in the house at all, God love him.'

'You've done very well,' said Liam. 'You shouldn't have gone to all this trouble.'

'If you couldn't do it for a neighbour like Mr Diamond — well? Forty-two years and there was never a cross word between us. A gentleman we always called him, Bertha and I. He kept himself to himself. Do you think can he hear us?' The old man did not move.

'How long has he been like this?' asked Liam.

'Just three days. He didn't bring in his milk one day and that's not like him, y'know. He'd left a key with Mrs Rankin, in case he'd ever lock himself out again — he did once, the wind blew the door shut — and she came in and found him like this in the chair downstairs. He was frozen, God love him. The doctor said it was a stroke.'

Liam nodded, looking at his father. He stood up and began edging the woman towards the bedroom door.

'I don't know how to thank you, Miss Hart. You've been more than good.'

'We got your address from your brother. Mrs Rankin phoned America on Tuesday.'

'Is he coming home?'

'He said he'd try. She said the line was as clear as a bell. It was like talking to next door. Yes, he said he'd try but he doubted it very much.' She had her hand on the door knob. 'Is that enough sandwiches?'

'Yes thanks, that's fine.' They stood looking at one another awkwardly. Liam fumbled in his pocket. 'Can I pay you for the ham . . . and the telegram?'

'I wouldn't dream of it,' she said. 'Don't insult me now, Liam.' He withdrew his hand from his pocket and smiled his thanks to her.

'It's late,' he said, 'perhaps you should go now and I'll sit up with him.'

'Very good. The priest was here earlier and gave him . . .' she groped for the word with her hands.

'Extreme Unction?'

'Yes. That's twice he has been in three days. Very attentive. Sometimes I think if our ministers were half as good . . . '

'Yes, but he wasn't what you could call gospel greedy.'

'He was lately,' she said.

'Changed times.'

She half turned to go and said, almost coyly,

'I'd hardly have known you with the beard.' She looked up at him, shaking her head in disbelief. He was trying to make her go, standing close to her but she skirted round him and went over to the bed. She touched the old man's shoulder.

'I'm away now, Mr Diamond. Liam is here. I'll see you in the morning,' she shouted into his ear. Then she was away.

Liam heard the old ladies' voices in the hallway below, then the slam of the front door. He heard the crackling of their feet over the frozen slush beneath the window. He lifted the tray off the chest of drawers and on to his knees. He hadn't realised it, but he was hungry. He ate the sandwiches and the piece of fruit cake, conscious of the chewing noise he was making with his mouth in the silence of the bedroom. There was little his father could do about it now. They used to have the most terrible rows about it. You'd have thought it was a matter of life and death. At table he had sometimes trembled with rage at the boys' eating habits, at their greed as he called it. At the noises they made, 'like cows getting out of muck'. After their mother had left them he took over the responsibility for everything. One night, as he served sausages from the pan Liam, not realising the filthy mood he was in, made a grab. His father in a sudden downward thrust jabbed the fork he had been using to cook the sausages into the back of Liam's hand.

'Control yourself.'

Four bright beads of blood appeared as Liam stared at them in disbelief.

'They'll remind you to use your fork in future.'

He was sixteen at the time.

The bedroom was cold and when he finally got round to drinking his tea it was tepid. He was annoyed that he couldn't heat it by pouring more. His feet were numb and felt damp. He went downstairs and put on his overcoat and brought the electric fire up to the bedroom, switching on both bars. He sat huddled over it, his fingers fanned out, trying to get warm. When the second bar was switched on there was a clicking noise and the smell of burning dust. He looked over at the bed but there was no movement.

'How do you feel?' he said again, not expecting an answer. For a long time he sat staring at the old man, whose breathing was audible but quiet – a kind of soft whistling in his nose. The alarm clock, its face bisected with a crack, said twelve-thirty. Liam checked it against the red figures of his digital watch. He stood up and went to the window. Outside the roofs tilted at white snow-covered angles. A faulty gutter hung spikes of icicles. There was no sound in the street, but from the main road came the distant hum of a late car that faded into silence.

He went out on to the landing and into what was his own bedroom. There was no bulb when he switched the light on so he took one from the hall and screwed it into the shadeless socket. The bed was there in the corner with its mattress of blue stripes. The lino was the same, with its square pock-marks showing other places the bed had been. The cheap green curtains that never quite met on their cord still did not meet.

He moved to the wall cupboard by the small fireplace and had to tug at the handle to get it open. Inside, the surface of everything had gone opaque with dust. Two old radios, one with a fretwork face, the other more modern with a tuning dial showing such places as Hilversum, Luxembourg, Athlone; a Dansette record player with its lid missing and its arm bent back, showing wires like severed nerves and blood vessels; the empty frame of the smashed glass picture was still there; several umbrellas, all broken. And there was his box of poster paints. He lifted it out and blew off the dust.

It was a large Quality Street tin and he eased the lid off, bracing it against his stomach muscles. The colours in the jars had shrunk to hard discs. Viridian green, vermilion, jonquil yellow. At the bottom of the box he found several sticks of charcoal, light in his fingers when he lifted them, warped. He dropped them into his pocket and put the tin back into the cupboard. There was a pile of magazines and papers and beneath that again he saw his large Winsor and Newton sketchbook. He eased it out and began to look through the work in it. Embarrassment was what he felt most, turning the pages, looking at the work of this schoolboy. He could see little talent in it, yet he realised he must have been good. There were several drawings of hands in red pastel which had promise. The rest of the pages were blank. He set the sketchbook aside to take with him and closed the door.

Looking round the room, it had to him the appearance of nakedness. He crouched and looked under the bed, but there was nothing there. His fingers coming in contact with the freezing lino made him aware how cold he was. His jaw was tight and he knew that if he relaxed he would shiver. He went back to his father's bedroom and sat down.

The old man had not changed his position. He had wanted him to be a lawyer or a doctor but Liam had insisted, although he had won a scholarship to the university, on going to art college. All that summer his father tried everything he knew to stop him. He tried to reason with him,

'*Be* something. And you can carry on doing your art. Art is O.K. as a sideline.'

But mostly he shouted at him. 'I've heard about these art students and what they get up to. Shameless bitches prancing

76

about with nothing on. And what sort of a job are you going to get? Drawing on pavements?' He nagged him every moment they were together about other things. Lying late in bed, the length of his hair, his outrageous appearance. Why hadn't he been like the other lads and got himself a job for the summer? It wasn't too late because he would willingly pay him if he came in and helped out in the shop.

One night, just as he was going to bed, Liam found the old framed print of cattle drinking. He had taken out the glass and had begun to paint on the glass itself with small tins of Humbrol enamel paints left over from aeroplane kits he had never finished. They produced a strange and exciting texture which was even better when the paint was viewed from the other side of the pane of glass. He sat stripped to the waist in his pyjama trousers painting a self-portrait reflected from the mirror on the wardrobe door. The creamy opaque nature of the paint excited him. It slid on to the glass, it built up, in places it ran scalloping like cinema curtains, and yet he could control it. He lost all track of time as he sat with his eyes focused on the face staring back at him and the painting he was trying to make of it. It became a face he had not known, the holes, the lines, the spots. He was in a new geography.

His brother and he used to play a game looking at each other's faces upside down. One lay on his back across the bed, his head flopped over the edge, reddening as the blood flooded into it. The other sat in a chair and stared at him. After a time the horror of seeing the eyes where the mouth should be, the inverted nose, the forehead gashed with red lips, would drive him to cover his eyes with his hands. 'It's your turn now,' he would say, and they would change places. It was like familiar words said over and over again until they became meaningless, and once he ceased to have purchase on the meaning of a word it became terrifying, an incantation. In adolescence he had come to hate his brother, could not

77

stand the physical presence of him, just as when he was lying upside down on the bed. It was the same with his father. He could not bear to touch him and yet for one whole winter when he had a bad shoulder he had to stay up late to rub him with oil of wintergreen. The old boy would sit with one hip on the bed and Liam would stand behind him, massaging the stinking stuff into the white flesh of his back. The smell, the way the blubbery skin moved under his fingers, made him want to be sick. No matter how many times he washed his hands, at school the next day he would still reek of oil of wintergreen.

It might have been the smell of the Humbrol paints or the strip of light under Liam's door – whatever it was, his father came in and yelled that it was half-past three in the morning and what the hell did he think he was doing, sitting half-naked drawing at this hour of the morning? He had smacked him full force with the flat of his hand on his bare back and, stung by the pain of it, Liam had leapt to retaliate. Then his father had started to laugh, a cold snickering laugh. 'Would you? Would you? Would you indeed?' he kept repeating with a smile pulled on his mouth and his fists bunched to knuckles in front of him. Liam retreated to the bed and his father turned on his heel and left. Thinking the incident over, Liam knotted his fists and cursed his father. He looked over his shoulder into the mirror and saw the primitive daub of his father's hand, splayed fingers outlined across his back. He heard him on the stairs and when he came back into the bedroom with the poker in his hand he felt his insides turn to water. But his father looked away from him with a sneer and smashed the painting to shards with one stroke. As he went out of the door he said,

'Watch your feet in the morning.'

He had never really 'left home'. It was more a matter of going to art college in London and not bothering to come back.

Almost as soon as he was away from the house his hatred for
his father eased. He simply stopped thinking about him. Of
late he had wondered if he was alive or dead – if he still had
the shop. The only communication they had had over the
years was when Liam sent him, not without a touch of
vindictiveness, an invitation to some of the openings of his
exhibitions.

Liam sat with his fingertips joined, staring at the old man.
It was going to be a long night. He looked at his watch and it
was only a little after two.

He paced up and down the room, listening to the tick of
snow on the window-pane. When he stopped to look down,
he saw it flurrying through the haloes of the street lamps. He
went into his own bedroom and brought back the sketchbook. He moved his chair to the other side of the bed so that
the light fell on his page. Balancing the book on his knee, he
began to draw his father's head with the stick of charcoal. It
made a light hiss each time a line appeared on the cartridge
paper. When drawing he always thought of himself as a wary
animal drinking, the way he looked up and down, up and
down, at his subject. The old man had failed badly. His head
scarcely dented the pillows, his cheeks were hollow and he
had not been shaved for some days. Earlier, when he had held
his hand it had been clean and dry and light like the hand of a
girl. The bedside light deepened the shadows of his face and
highlighted the rivulets of veins on his temple. It was a long
time since he had used charcoal and he became engrossed in
the way it had to be handled and the different subtleties of
line he could get out of it. He loved to watch a drawing
develop before his eyes.

His work had been well received and among the small
Dublin art world he was much admired – justly he thought.
But some critics had scorned his work as 'cold' and 'formalist'
– one had written, 'Like Mondrian except that he can't draw a
straight line' – and this annoyed him because it was precisely

what he was trying to do. He felt it was unfair to be criticised for succeeding in his aims.

His father began to cough – a low wet bubbling sound. Liam leaned forward and touched the back of his hand gently. Was this man to blame in any way? Or had he only himself to blame for the shambles of his life? He had married once and lived with two other women. At present he was on his own. Each relationship had ended in hate and bitterness, not because of drink or lack of money or any of the usual reasons but because of a mutual nauseating dislike.

He turned the page and began to draw the old man again. The variations in tone from jet black to pale grey, depending on the pressure he used, fascinated him. The hooded lids of the old man's eyes, the fuzz of hair sprouting from the ear next the light, the darkness of the partially open mouth. Liam made several more drawings, absorbed, working slowly, refining the line of each until it was to his satisfaction. He was pleased with what he had done. At art school he had loved the life class better than any other. It never ceased to amaze him how sometimes it could come just right, better than he had hoped for; the feeling that something was working through him to produce a better work than at first envisaged.

Then outside he heard the sound of an engine followed by the clinking of milk bottles. When he looked at his watch he was amazed to see that it was five-thirty. He leaned over to speak to his father,

'Are you all right?'

His breathing was not audible and when Liam touched his arm it was cold. His face was cold as well. He felt for his heart, slipping his hand inside his pyjama jacket, but could feel nothing. He was dead. His father. He was dead and the slackness of his dropped jaw disturbed his son. In the light of the lamp his dead face looked like the open-mouthed moon. Liam wondered if he should tie it up before it set. In a

Pasolini film he had seen Herod's jaw being trussed and he wondered if he was capable of doing it for his father.

Then he saw himself in his hesitation, saw the lack of any emotion in his approach to the problem. He was aware of the deadness inside himself and felt helpless to do anything about it. It was why all his women had left him. One of them accused him of making love the way other people rodded drains.

He knelt down beside the bed and tried to think of something good from the time he had spent with his father. Anger and sneers and nagging was all that he could picture. He knew he was grateful for his rearing but he could not *feel* it. If his father had not been there somebody else would have done it. And yet it could not have been easy – a man left with two boys and a business to run. He had worked himself to a sinew in his tobacconist's, opening at seven in the morning to catch the workers and closing at ten at night. Was it for his boys that he worked so hard? The man was in the habit of earning and yet he never spent. He had even opened for three hours on Christmas Day.

Liam stared at the dead drained face and suddenly the mouth held in that shape reminded him of something pleasant. It was the only joke his father had ever told and to make up for the smallness of his repertoire he had told it many times; of two ships passing in mid-Atlantic. He always megaphoned his hands to tell the story.

'Where are you bound for?' shouts one captain.

'Rio – de – Janeir – io. Where are you bound for?'

And the other captain, not to be outdone, yells back,

'Cork – a – lork – a – lor – io.'

When he had finished the joke he always repeated the punch-line, laughing and nodding in disbelief that something could be so funny.

'Cork a – lorka – lorio.'

Liam found that his eyes had filled with tears. He tried to

keep them coming but they would not. In the end he had to close his eyes and a tear spilled from his left eye on to his cheek. It was small and he wiped it away with a crooked index finger.

He stood up from the kneeling position and closed the sketchbook, which was lying open on the bed. He might work on the drawings later. Perhaps a charcoal series. He walked to the window. Dawn would not be up for hours yet. In America it would be daylight and his brother would be in shirtsleeves. He would have to wait until Mrs Rankin was up before he could phone him – and the doctor would be needed for a death certificate. There was nothing he could do at the moment, except perhaps tie up the jaw. The Miss Harts when they arrived would know everything that ought to be done.

Phonefun Limited

WHEN SHE HEARD the whine of the last customer's fast spin – a bearded student with what seemed like a year's supply of Y-fronts – Sadie Thompson changed her blue nylon launderette coat for her outdoor one and stood jingling the keys by the door until he left. It was dark and wet and the streets reflected the lights from the shop windows. She had to rush to get to the Spar before it closed, and was out of breath – not that she had much to buy, potatoes, sugar and tea-bags. In the corner shop she got her cigarettes, the evening paper and a copy of *Men Only*, which she slipped inside the newspaper and put in her carrier bag. She slowly climbed the steep street in darkness because the Army had put out most of the street lights. She turned in at Number Ninety-six. The door stuck momentarily on a large envelope lying on the mat.

She had the table set and the dinner ready for Agnes when she came in.

'Hello, Sadie, love,' she said and kissed her on the cheek. Beside Sadie, Agnes was huge. She wore an expensive silver-fox fur coat. Sadie did not like the coat and had said so. It was much too much for a woman whose only job was cleaning the local primary school.

'I'm knackered,' said Agnes, kicking off her shoes and falling into the armchair. There was a hole in the toe of her tights.

'Take off your coat, your dinner's ready,' said Sadie.

'Hang on. Let me have a fag first.'

She lit up a cigarette and put her head back in the chair. Sadie thought she looked a putty colour. She was grossly overweight but would do nothing about it, no matter what Sadie said.

'Are you all right?'

'I'll be all right in a minute. It's that bloody hill. It's like entering the Olympics.'

'If you ask me, you're carrying too much weight. When did you last weigh yourself?'

'This morning.'

'And what were you?'

'I don't know,' said Agnes laughing, 'I was afraid to look.'

With her head back like that her fat neck and chin were one. There were red arcs of lipstick on the cork-tip of her cigarette. Sadie served the mash and sausages.

'Sit over,' she said. Agnes stubbed her cigarette out and, groaning for effect, came to the table still wearing her coat.

'You'd think to hear you that you'd cleaned that school by yourself.'

'It feels like I did.' Agnes raised her fork listlessly to her mouth. 'Did the post come?'

'Yes.'

'Much?'

'It feels fat.'

'Aw God no.'

'You'll have to brighten up a bit. Don't be so glum.'

'God, that's a good one coming from you, Sadie. I don't think I've seen you smiling since Christmas.'

'I'm the brains. You're supposed to be the charm. I don't *have* to smile.' They ate in silence except for the sound of their forks making small screeches against the plate.

'I wish you'd take off your coat when you're eating. It looks that slovenly,' said Sadie. Agnes heaved herself to her feet, took off her coat and flung it on the sofa. She turned on the transistor. The news was on so she tuned it to some music.

'I need a wee doze before I brighten up. You know that, Sadie.'

'I suppose I'm not tired after a day in that bloody laundry-ette?'

Agnes nibbled her sausage at the front of her closed mouth, very quickly, like a rabbit. The music on the radio stopped and a foreign voice came on and babbled.

'That's a great programme you picked.'

'It's better than the Northern Ireland news.'

The foreign voice stopped and music came on again. Agnes finished what was on her plate.

'Is there anything for afters?'

'You can open some plums if you want.'

Agnes lurched out to the tiled kitchen and opened a tin of plums. She threw the circle of lid into the bucket and came back with the tin and a spoon.

'It's cold on your feet out there. There's a draught coming in under that door that would clean corn.' She ate the plums from the tin. Some juice trickled on to her chin.

'Want some?' She offered the half-finished tin to Sadie, but she refused.

'It's no wonder you're fat.'

'It oils my voice. Makes it nice for the phone.'

'I got you a *Men Only* if you run out of inspiration. It's there on the sideboard.'

'Thanks, love, but I don't think I'll need it.' Agnes drank off the last of the juice from the tin.

'You'll cut your lip one of these days,' said Sadie, 'don't say I didn't warn you.'

Agnes lit a cigarette and rolled one across the table to Sadie. She dropped the dead match into the tin.

'That was good,' she said. 'I'm full to the gunnels.' She slapped her large stomach with the flat of her hand in satisfaction. The foreigner began to speak gobbledegook again.

'Aw shut up,' said Sadie. 'Men are all the same no matter what they're speaking.' She twiddled the knob until she got another station with music. Almost immediately the music stopped and a man with a rich American drawl began to speak.

'Aw God, Sadie, do you remember the Yanks? He sounds just like one I had.'

'Will I ever forget them? They could spend money all right.'

'That's exactly like his voice. It's the spit of him.'

'Give us a light.' Agnes leaned over and touched Sadie's cigarette with her own. Sadie pulled hard until it was lit.

'I fancied him no end,' said Agnes. 'He was lovely. I think it was his first time but he pretended it wasn't.'

'I think you told me about him.'

'My Yankee Doodle Dandy, I called him. I can still feel the stubble of his haircut. It was like he had sandpapered up the back of his neck. Blondie. We sort of went together for a while.'

'You mean he didn't pay.'

'That kind of thing.'

'Better clear this table.' Sadie put the cigarette in her mouth, closing one eye against the trickle of blue smoke and began to remove the dirty plates. Ash toppled on to the cloth. She came back from the kitchen and gently brushed the grey roll into the palm of her other hand and dropped it into Agnes's tin. Agnes said,

'You wash and I'll dry.'

'What you mean is I'll wash and put them in the rack and then about ten o'clock you'll come out and put them in the cupboard.'

'Well, it's more hygienic that way. I saw in the paper that the tea-towel leaves germs all over them.'

'You only read what suits you.'

Sadie went out into the kitchen to wash up the dishes. She heard the programme on the radio finish and change to a service with an American preacher. It kept fading and going out of focus and was mixed up with pips of Morse Code. When she had finished she washed out the tea-towel in some Lux and hung it in the yard to dry. She could do her own washing at the launderette but she hated lugging the bagful of damp clothes home. There was such a weight in wet clothes. If she did that too often she would end up with arms like a chimpanzee. When she went back into the living room Agnes was asleep in her armchair beside the radio with a silly smile on her face.

Sadie picked up the large envelope off the sideboard and opened it with her thumb and spilled out the pile of envelopes on to the table. She began to open them and separate the cheques and money. On each letter she marked down the amount of money contained and then set it to one side. Agnes began to snore wetly, her head pitched forward on to her chest. When she had all the letters opened, Sadie got up and switched off the radio. In the silence Agnes woke with a start. Sadie said,

'So you're back with us again.'

'What do you mean?'

'You were sound asleep.'

'I was not. I was only closing my eyes. Just for a minute.'

'You were snoring like a drunk.'

'Indeed I was not. I was just resting my eyes.'

The ticking of the clock annoyed Agnes so she switched the radio on again just in time to hear 'The Lord is my Shepherd' being sung in a smooth American drawl. She tuned it to Radio One. Sadie said,

'Hymns give me the creeps. That Billy Graham one. Euchh!' She shuddered. 'You weren't in Belfast for the Blitz, were you?'

'No, I was still a nice country girl from Cookstown. My

87

Americans all came from the camp out at Larrycormack. That's where my Yankee Doodle Dandy was stationed. You stuck it out here through the Blitz?'

'You can say that again. We all slept on the Cavehill for a couple of nights. Watched the whole thing. It was terrible – fires everywhere.'

'Sadie, will you do my hair?'

Sadie took the polythene bag bulging with rollers from under the table and began combing Agnes's hair.

'It needs to be dyed again. Your roots is beginning to show.'

'I think I'll maybe grow them out this time. Have it greying at the temples.'

Sadie damped each strand of hair and rolled it up tight into Agnes's head, then fixed it with a hairpin. With each tug of the brush Agnes let her head jerk with it.

'I love somebody working with my hair. It's so relaxing.' Sadie couldn't answer because her mouth was bristling with hairpins. Agnes said,

'How much was there in the envelopes?'

'Hengy-hee oung.'

'How much?'

Sadie took the hairpins from her mouth.

'Sixty-eight pounds.'

'That's not bad at all.'

'You're right there. It's better than walking the streets on a night like this.'

'If it goes on like this I'm going to give up my job in that bloody school.'

'I think you'd be foolish. Anything could happen. It could all fall through any day.'

'How could it?'

'I don't know. It all seems too good to be true. The Post Office could catch on. Even the Law. Or the tax man.'

'It's not against the law?'

88

'I wouldn't be too sure.'

'It's against the law the other way round but not the way we do it.'

'There. That's you finished,' said Sadie, giving the rollers a final pat in close to her head. She held the mirror up for Agnes to see but before she put it away she looked at herself. Her neck was a dead give away. That's where the age really showed. You could do what you liked with make-up on your face but there was no way of disguising those chicken sinews on your neck. And the back of the hands. They showed it too. She put the mirror on the mantelpiece and said,

'Are you ready, Agnes?'

'Let's have a wee gin first.'

'O.K.'

She poured two gins and filled them to the brim with tonic. Agnes sat over to the table. When she drank her gin she pinched in her mouth with the delightful bitterness.

'Too much gin,' she said.

'You say that every time.'

Agnes sipped some more out of her glass and then topped up with tonic. She began to sort through the letters. She laughed and nodded her head at some. At others she turned down the corners of her mouth.

'I suppose I better make a start.'

She lifted the telephone and set it beside her on the table. She burst out laughing.

'Have you read any of these, Sadie?'

'No.'

'Listen to this. "Dear Samantha, you really turn me on with that sexy voice of yours. Not only me but my wife as well. I get her to listen on the extension. Sometimes it's too much for the both of us." Good Gawd. I never thought there was any women listening to me.' She picked up the phone and snuggled it between her ear and the fat of her shoulder.

'Kick over that pouffe, Sadie.'

Sadie brought the pouffe to her feet. Agnes covered the hole in the toe of her tights with the sole of her other foot. She sorted through the letters and chose one.

' "Available at any time." He must be an oul' batchelor. O three one. That's Edinburgh isn't it? Dirty oul' kilty.'

She dialled the number and while she listened to the dialling tone she smiled at Sadie. She raised her eyebrows as if she thought she was posh. A voice answered at the other end. Agnes's voice changed into a soft purr which pronounced its -ings.

'Hello is Ian there? . . . Oh, I didn't recognise your voice. This is Samantha . . . Yes, I can hold on, but not too long.' She covered the mouthpiece with her hand and, exaggerating her lips, said to Sadie,

'The egg-timer.'

Sadie went out to the kitchen and came back with it. It was a cheap plastic one with pink sand. She set it on the table with the full side on top.

'Ah, there you are again, honey,' whispered Agnes into the mouthpiece, 'are you all ready now? Good. What would you like to talk about? . . . Well, I'm lying here on my bed. It's a lovely bed with black silk sheets . . . No, it has really. Does that do something for you? Mmm, it's warm. I have the heating turned up full. It's so warm all I am wearing are my undies . . . Lemon . . . Yes, and the panties are lemon too . . . All right, if you insist . . .' Agnes put the phone down on the table and signalled to Sadie to light her a fag. She made a rustling noise with her sleeve close to the mouthpiece then picked up the phone again.

'There, I've done what you asked . . . You're not normally breathless, are you, Ian? Have you just run up the stairs? . . . No, I'm only kidding . . . I know only too well what it's like to have asthma.'

She listened for a while, taking the lit cigarette from Sadie.

She rolled her eyes to heaven and smiled across the table at her. She covered the mouthpiece with her hand.

'He's doing his nut.'

Sadie topped up her gin and tonic from the gin bottle.

'Do you really want me to do that? That might cost a little more money . . . All right, just for you love.' She laughed heartily and paused. 'Yes, I'm doing it now . . . Yes, it's fairly pleasant. A bit awkward . . . Actually I'm getting to like it. Ohhh, I love it now . . . Say what again? . . . Ohhh, I love it.'

She turned to Sadie.

'He's rung off. That didn't take long. He just came and went. Who's next?'

Sadie flicked another letter to her.

'London,' she said. 'Jerome. Only on Thursdays after eight.'

'That's today. Probably the wife's night out at the Bingo.'

She dialled the number and when a voice answered she said,

'Hello Jerome, this is Samantha.'

Sadie turned over the egg-timer.

'Oh, sorry love – say that again. Ger – o – mey. I thought it was Ger – ome. Like Ger-ome Cairns, the song writer. Would you like to talk or do you want me to . . . O.K., fire away . . . I'm twenty-four . . . Blonde . . . Lemon, mostly . . . Yes, as brief as possible. Sometimes they're so brief they cut into me.' She listened for a moment, then covering the mouthpiece said to Sadie,

'This one's disgusting. How much did he pay?'

Sadie looked at the letter.

'Ten pounds. Don't lose him. Do what he says.'

'Yes, this is still Samantha.' Her voice went babyish and her mouth pouted. 'How could a nice little girl like me do a thing like that? . . . Well, if it pleases you.' Agnes lifted her stubby finger and wobbled it wetly against her lips. 'Can you

91

hear that? . . . Yes, I like it . . . Yes, I have *very* long legs.'
She lifted her legs off the pouffe and looked at them dis-
approvingly. She had too many varicose veins. She'd had
them out twice.

'You *are* a bold boy, but your time is nearly up.' The last of
the pink sand was caving in and trickling through. Sadie
raised a warning finger then signalled with all ten. She
mouthed,

'Ten pounds. Don't lose him.'

'All right, just for you . . . Then I'll have to go,' said
Agnes and she wobbled her finger against her lips again. 'Is
that enough? . . . You just write us another letter. You know
the box number? Good . . . I love you too, Ger – o – mey,
Bye-eee.' She put the phone down.

'For God's sake give us another gin,' she said. 'What a
creep!'

'It's better than walking the street,' said Sadie. 'What I
like about it is that they can't get near you.'

'Catch yourself on, Sadie. If anyone got near us now they'd
run a mile.'

'I used to be frightened of them. Not all the time. But
there was one every so often that made your scalp crawl.
Something not right about them. Those ones gave me the
heemy-jeemies, I can tell you. You felt you were going to end
up in an entry somewhere – strangled – with your clothes
over your head.'

Agnes nodded in agreement. 'Or worse,' she said.

Sadie went on, 'When I think of the things I've had to
endure. Do you remember that pig that gave me the
kicking? I was in hospital for a fortnight. A broken arm
and a ruptured spleen – the bastard.'

Agnes began to laugh. 'Do you remember the time
I broke my ankle? Jumping out of a lavatory window.
Gawd, I was sure and certain I was going to be murdered
that night.'

'Was that the guy with the steel plate in his head?'

'The very one. He said he would go mad if I didn't stroke it for him.'

'What?'

'His steel plate.'

'I can still smell some of those rooms. It was no picnic, Agnes, I can tell you.'

'The only disease you can get at this game is an ear infection. Who's next?'

Sadie passed another letter to her.

'Bristol, I think.'

'This one wants *me* to breathe. Good God, what will they think of next?'

'I hate their guts, every last one of them.'

'Do you fancy doing this one?' asked Agnes.

'No. You know I'm no good at it.'

'Chrissake, Sadie, you can breathe. I never get a rest. Why's it always me?'

'Because I told you. You are the creative one. I just look after the books. The business end. Would you know how to go about putting an ad in? Or wording it properly? Or getting a box number? You stick to the bit you're good at. You're really great, you know. I don't know how you think the half of them up.'

Agnes smiled. She wiggled her stubby toes on the pouffe. She said,

'Do you know what I'd like? With the money.'

'What? Remember that we're still paying off that carpet in the bedroom — and the suite. Don't forget the phone bills either.'

'A jewelled cigarette holder. Like the one Audrey Hepburn had in that picture — what was it called?'

'*The Nun's Story?*'

'No.'

'*Breakfast at Tiffany's?*'

'Yes, one like that. I could use it on the phone. It'd make me feel good.'

As Agnes dialled another number Sadie said,

'You're mad in the skull.'

'We can afford it. Whisht now.'

When the phone was answered at the other end she said,

'Hello, Samantha here,' and began to breathe loudly into the receiver. She quickened her pace gradually until she was panting, then said,

'He's hung up. Must have been expecting me. We should get a pair of bellows for fellas like him. Save my puff.'

'I'll go up and turn the blanket on, then we'll have a cup of tea,' said Sadie. Agnes turned another letter towards herself and dialled a number.

Upstairs Sadie looked round the bedroom with admiration. She still hadn't got used to it. The plush almost ankle-deepness of the mushroom-coloured carpet and the brown flock wallpaper, the brown duvet with the matching brown sheets. The curtains were of heavy velvet and were the most luxurious stuff she had ever touched. She switched on the blanket and while on her hands and knees she allowed her fingers to sink into the pile of the carpet. All her life she had wanted a bedroom like this. Some of the places she had lain down, she wouldn't have kept chickens in. She heard Agnes's voice coming blurred from downstairs. She owed a lot to her. Everything, in fact. From the first time they met, the night they were both arrested and ended up in the back of the same paddy-wagon, she had thought there was something awful good about her, something awful kind. She had been so good-looking in her day too, tall and stately and well-built. They had stayed together after that night – all through the hard times. As Agnes said, once you quit the streets it didn't qualify you for much afterwards. Until lately, when she had shown this amazing talent for talking on the phone. It had all started one night when a man got the wrong number and

Agnes had chatted him up until he was doing his nut at the other end. They had both crouched over the phone wheezing and laughing their heads off at the puffs and pants of him. Then it was Sadie's idea to put the whole thing on a commercial basis and form the Phonefun company. She dug her fingers into the carpet and brushed her cheek against the crisp sheet.

'Agnes,' she said and went downstairs to make the tea.

She stood waiting for the kettle to boil, then transferred the tea-bag from one cup of boiling water to the other. Agnes laughed loudly at something in the living room. Sadie heard her say,

'But if I put the phone there you'll not hear me.'

She put some custard creams on a plate and brought the tea in.

'Here you are, love,' she said, setting the plate beside the egg-timer. 'He's over his time.' Agnes covered the mouthpiece and said,

'I forgot to start it.' Then back to the phone. 'I can get some rubber ones if you want me to . . . But you'll have to pay for them. Will you send the money through? . . . Gooood boy. Now I really must go . . . Yes, I'm listening.' She made a face, half laughing, half in disgust, to Sadie. 'Well done, love . . . Bye-eee, sweetheart.' She puckered her mouth and did a kiss noise into the mouthpiece, then put the phone down.

'Have your tea now, Agnes, you can do the others later.'

'There's only two more I can do tonight. The rest have special dates.'

'You can do those. Then we'll go to bed. Eh?'

'O.K.,' said Agnes. 'Ahm plumb tuckered out.'

'You're what?'

'Plumb tuckered out. It's what my Yankee Doodle Dandy used to say afterwards.'

'What started you on *him* tonight?'

'I don't know. I just remembered, that's all. He used to bring me nylons and put them on for me.'

She fiddled with the egg-timer and allowed the pink sand to run through it. She raised her legs off the pouffe and turned her feet outwards, looking at them.

'I don't like tights,' she said, 'I read somewhere they're unhygienic.'

'Do you want to hear the news before we go up? Just in case?'

'Just in case what?'

'They could be rioting all over the city and we wouldn't know a thing.'

'You're better not to know, even if they are. That tea's cold.'

'That's because you didn't drink it. You talk far too much.'

Agnes drank her tea and snapped a custard cream in half with her front teeth.

'I don't think I'll bother with these next two.'

'That's the way you lose customers. If you phone them once they'll come back for more – and for a longer time. Give them a short time. Keep them interested.' She lifted the crumbed plate and the cups and took them out to the kitchen. Agnes lit another cigarette and sat staring vacantly at the egg-timer. She said without raising her eyes,

'Make someone happy with a phone call.'

'I'm away on up,' said Sadie. 'I'll keep a place warm for you.'

Sadie was in bed when Agnes came up.

'Take your rollers out,' she said.

Agnes undressed, grunting and tugging hard at her roll-on. When she got it off she gave a long sigh and rubbed the puckered flesh that had just been released.

'That's like taking three Valium, to get out of that,' she said. She sat down on the side of the bed and began taking her

96

rollers out, clinking the hairpins into a saucer on the dressing table. Sadie spoke from the bed,

'Were you really in love with that Yank?'

'Yes, as near as possible.'

Agnes shook her hair loose and rolled back into bed. She turned out the light and Sadie notched into her back. She began to stroke Agnes's soft upper arm, then moved to her haunch.

'I've got a bit of a headache, love,' said Agnes.

Sadie turned to the wall and Agnes felt her harsh skin touch her own.

'My God, Sadie,' she said, 'you've got heels on you like pumice stones.'

The Daily Woman

S HE WOKE LIKE a coiled spring, her head pressed on to the mattress, the knot of muscle at the side of her jaw taut, holding her teeth together. The texture of her cheeks felt tight and shiny from the tears she had cried as she had determined herself to sleep the night before. She lay for a moment trying to sense whether he was behind her or not, but knowing he wasn't. The baby was still asleep. She could tell by the slight squeaking movement of the pram springs from the foot of the bed whether it was asleep or not. The house was silent. She was a good baby. When she woke in the mornings she kicked her legs for hours. Only once in a while she cried.

Liz got up and went to the bathroom. In the mirror she saw where he had snapped the shoulder strap of her slip. It looked like a cheap off-the-shoulder evening dress. She examined her face, touching it with her fingertips. It had not bruised. He must be losing his touch. Her mouth still tasted of blood and she tested the looseness of her teeth with her index finger and thumb.

When she heard Paul thumping the sides of his cot she quickly finished her washing and went in to him. She tested if he was dry.

'Good for you,' she said. He was coming three and a half but she couldn't trust him a single night without a nappy.

She gave him his handful of Ricicles on the pillow and he lay down beside them with a smile, looking at them, picking them up with concentration and eating them one by one like sweets. She went back to the kitchen and began heating the baby's bottle. The cold of the lino made her walk on tip-toe and she stood on the small mat, holding her bare elbows and shivering while the water came to the boil. She hated waiting — especially for a short time. Waiting a long time, you could be lazy or do something if you felt like it. She saw last night's dishes congealed in the sink, the fag-ends, but had no time or desire to do anything about it. In short waits she was aware of the rubbish of her life.

After the milk heated and while the bottle was cooling in a pot of cold water, she looked into the front room. Light came through the gap in the curtains. Eamonn lay on his back on the sofa, his shoes kicked off, breathing heavily through his slack open mouth. When she came back after feeding and changing the baby, he was still in the same position. She whacked the curtains open loudly. His eyes cringed and wavered and he turned his face into the sofa. He closed and opened his mouth and from where she stood she could hear the tacky dryness of it.

'Fuck you,' he said.

He lay there as she tidied around him. On the cream tiled hearth a complete cigarette had become a worm of white ash on brown sweat.

In the kitchen she began to wash up and make a cup of tea. They had run out of bread except for a heel of pan. She opened a packet of biscuits.

'Liz,' Eamonn called her. 'Liz.'

But she didn't feel like answering. She went and picked Paul out of his cot and let him run into the front room to annoy his Daddy. When she was sitting at her tea Eamonn came in, his shirt-tail out, and drank several cups of water. He looked wretched.

'There's a sliding brick in my head,' he said. 'Every time I move it wallops.'

Still she said nothing. He shuffled towards her and she looked out of the window at the corrugated-iron coal-house and the other pre-fabs stretching up the hill.

'Let me see,' he said and turned her face with the back of his hand. 'You're all right.'

'No thanks to you,' she said. The ridiculous thing was that *she* felt sorry for *him*. How could anyone do that to her? How could anyone knock her to the floor and kick her, then take off his shoes and fall asleep? Why did she feel pity for him and not for herself? He sat down on a stool and held on to his head.

'I suppose you don't remember anything,' she said.

'Enough.'

'I'll not stand much more of it, Eamonn.'

'Don't talk shit.' He wasn't angry. It was just his way. Sober she could handle him. The next day he never apologised – not once, and she had learned not to expect it. Last night he had got it into his head that the baby wasn't his. This was new and she had been frightened that in drink he might do something to it, so she had let him work out his anger on her.

Only she knew it was a possibility. Those nights had been long, sitting on her own minding her child, bored to tears with television, so that when Barney started to call – she had known him since her days in primary school – it had been a gradual and easy fall. He worked in a garage and was a folk singer of sorts. He made her feel relaxed in his company and she laughed, which was unusual for her. Even while they were at it behind the snibbed door of their small bathroom he could make her laugh – his head almost touching one wall while he got movement on her by levering his sock soles off the other.

Then he just stopped calling, saying that he was getting more and more engagements for his folk group. But that was nearly two years ago and she was disturbed that she should start being hit for it now. She wondered who had put it into his mind. Was it a rumour in that Provos club where he spent the most of his time drinking? God knows what else he got up to there. Once he had brought home an armful of something wrapped in sacking and hid it in the roof-space. When she pestered him as to what it was he refused to tell her.

'It's only for a couple of nights,' was all he would say. Those two days she fretted herself sick waiting for an Army-pig to pull up at the door.

Liz threw her tea down the sink.

'I suppose there's no money left,' she said, looking out the window. He made a kind of snort laugh. 'What am I going to use for the messages?'

'Henderson pays you today, doesn't he?'

'Jesus, you drink your dole money and I work to pay the messages. That's lovely. Smashin'.'

Paul had wandered in from the other room, shredding the cork tip of a cigarette butt, and Eamonn began to talk to him, ignoring her.

'Mucky pup,' he said taking it from between the child's fingers and roughly brushing them clean with his own hand.

'That's right, just throw it on the floor at your arse. I'm here to clean it up,' shouted Liz. She began thumpingly to wash the dishes. Eamonn went to the bathroom.

The hill to Ardview House was so steep that the pram handle pressed against the chest muscles just beneath her small breasts. Liz angled herself, pushing with her chest rather than her arms. It was a hot autumn day and the lack of wind made her feel breathless. Half way up she stopped and put the brake on with her foot.

'Paul,' she said, panting, 'get off, son, before I have a coronary.'

The child girned that he didn't want to but she was firm

with him, lifting him under the armpits and setting him on the ground.

'You can hold on to the handle.'

In the pram, sheltered by its black hood, the baby was a pink knitted bonnet, its face almost obscured by a bobbing dummy. She continued up the hill.

She seemed to be doing this journey all the time, day in day out, up and down this hill. She knew where the puddles were in the worn tarmac of the footpath and could avoid them even though she was unsighted by the pram. A police car bounced over the crest of the hill, its lights flashing and its siren screaming. It passed her with a whumph of speed and gradually faded into the distance, spreading ripples of nervousness as far as the ear could hear.

When she turned off the road into the gravelled driveway she noticed that there was jam or marmalade on the black pram-hood. She wiped it with a tissue, but the smear still glistened. She wet her finger and rubbed it, but only succeeded in making her fingers tacky. The pram was impossible to push on the gravel and she pulled it the rest of the way to the house. Paul was running ahead, hurrying to get to the playroom. The Henderson children had left a legacy of broken but expensive toys and usually Paul disappeared and gave her little trouble until she had her work finished.

She wondered if Mr Henderson would be in. She was nervous of him, not just because he was her boss, but because of the way he looked at her. Of late he seemed to wait around in the mornings until she came. And then there was the money business.

Henderson was a big-wig who had made his money in paints, and on rare occasions when there were more than six guests his wife would invite Liz to dress up a bit and come and help serve dinner. Although a Unionist through and through, Henderson liked to be able to say that he employed Catholics.

'It's the only way forward. We must begin to build bridges. Isn't that right, Mrs O'Prey?' he'd say over his shoulder as she cleared the soup plates.

'Yes, sir,' said Liz.

In his house the other guests nodded.

'I make no secret of it. It's my ambition to become Lord Mayor of this town. Get others to put into practice what I preach.'

As she washed the dishes in her best dress she heard them laugh and guffaw in the other room.

The baby was sleeping, so Liz left her at the front door in the warm sunlight and went down to the pantry where she kept her cleaning things. She heard a door close upstairs and a moment later Mr Henderson came into the kitchen. He looked as if he had just had a shower and his hair, which was normally bushy, lay slick and black against the skin of his head. He wore a sage-green towelling dressing-gown knotted at the waist. His legs were pallid and hairy and he wore a pair of backless clog slippers. Standing with his back to her his heels were raw red.

'Good morning, Mrs O'Prey.'

She nodded at his back, Vim in one hand, J-cloths in the other, and excused herself. But he put himself between her and the door.

'That's a pleasant morning,' he said. 'Hot, even.'

She agreed. He bent to the refrigerator, blocking her way. He poured himself a glass of orange juice and leaned his back against the breakfast bar. He was tall and thin, in the region of fifty, but she found it hard to tell age. He wasn't ugly but she wouldn't have called him good-looking. His face had the grey colour of someone not long awake and his eyes behind dark-rimmed spectacles had the same look.

'How are things?'

'All right,' she said.

'Have you thought about my proposition?'

'Eh?'

'Did you think about my offer?'

'No,' she said and edged past him to the door to go upstairs. She began by cleaning the bathroom, hoping that Mr Henderson would leave for work before she would make the beds. She put his denture powder back in the cabinet and returned his toothbrush to the rack. She hosed round the shower with the sprinkler and with finger and thumb lifted a small scribbled clot of his black hairs which refused to go down the rose grating and dropped them into the toilet bowl. The noise of the flush must have camouflaged his footsteps on the stairs because Liz, squatting to clean some talc which had spilled down the outside of the bath, did not notice him standing in the doorway until he spoke.

'How remarkably thin you keep,' he said. She did not look round but was aware of a large gap between her jumper at the back and her jeans tight on her hips.

'It's hard work that does it.' She tried to tug her jumper down. He probably saw right into her pants. Let him. She turned round, her elbow resting on the lavatory seat. 'And not eating too much.'

'Oh, Mrs Henderson asked me to pay you this week.' He slippered off to his bedroom and came back a moment later with a wallet. He sat on the edge of the bath. If Liz was to sit the only place was the lavatory, so she stood while he drew clean notes from the wallet.

'She was in a rush this morning going out. How much is it?'

Liz told him and he counted out the twelve pounds. He set the money on the Vanitory unit, then went on taking out notes. Blue ones, slightly hinged from the bend of the wallet. Five – ten – fifteen she saw him mouth. He stopped at seventy-five. A strand of his damp hair detached itself from the rest and hung like a black sickle in his eye. He looked at her.

'I can afford it,' he said. 'It's yours if you want it.'

She could see herself reflected from neck to knees in a rectangular mirror that ran the length of the bath. Would he never give up? This was a rise of twenty-five from the last time. She remembered once up an entry doing a pee standing up for thruppence and the boys had whooped and jeered as she splashed her good shoes and had run off and never paid her. Afterwards she had cried.

'I can afford better but I want you,' he said. 'It will be on the desk in my room.' His voice was hoarse and slightly trembling because she had not said no. He moved towards his room, saying over his shoulder, 'I'm not going in to the office this morning.'

Liz heard the one-stair-at-a-time stomp of Paul and went to the door to meet him.

'Muh,' he said.

'Yes, love.' She could feel the shake in her knees as she carried him down the stairs.

She began to scrape and put the accumulated dishes into the dishwasher. The bin yawned with bad breath when Paul pushed the foot-pedal with his hand so she emptied it and cleaned it with bleach. At the sink the wingbones of her pelvis touched the stainless steel of the sink and she winced. She must have bruised. Eamonn would probably have gone back to bed now that he had it all to himself. He would get up about mid-day and go to either the pub or the bookies. Probably both. They were next door, the one feeding off the other. She had noticed a horseshoe of wear in the pavement from one door to the other. At night he would go to the Provos club. The drink was cheaper there because most of it was hi-jacked. He would not be home until midnight at the earliest and there was no guarantee they wouldn't have another boxing match. She breathed out and heard it as a shuddering sigh.

'Muh,' Paul said.

'Yes, love, whatever you say.'

What could she do with that kind of money? Eamonn would know immediately – he could smell pound notes – and want to know how she got it. If she got a new rig-out it would be the same. He would kill her. Before or after she had spent the money didn't matter. Her mother had always harped on that Liz had married beneath her.

She wiped down the white Formica and began to load the washing machine from the laundry basket. Or toys or kids. She could think of no way of spending where questions wouldn't be asked. At eleven she made a coffee. She opened a window and smoked a cigarette, sharpening its ash on a flowered saucer.

'Buh?' Paul asked, reaching her a pot lid.

'Thanks, son.' She took it off him and set it on the table.

When Liz reached three-quarters' way down her cigarette she stubbed it out with determination, bending it almost double. She got up and brought Paul with a biscuit and milk in his baby cup into the playroom.

'There's a good boy,' she said. 'Mammy will be cross if you come out.'

She had walloped him round the legs before for keeping her back with her work, so he knew what was in store for him if he wandered. She went outside and checked the baby in the pram. She was still asleep, so she closed the front door quietly and climbed the stairs.

In his room Mr Henderson sat at a small desk strewn with papers. At her knock he raised his glasses to his hairline and turned.

'Yes?'

'It's me.'

'Well?'

'All right,' she said. Her voice caught in her throat as if she had been crying for a long time. 'Just so long as you don't kiss me.'

'That will not be necessary.' His face broke into a frightened smile of disbelief. He was still in his dressing-gown, a furry thigh sticking out. He came to her, his arm extended — fatherly almost.

'You're sure? I would get very angry if you were to change your mind once we had started.'

She nodded. 'What do you want me to do?'

'I want you to lie down.' That was a favourite song of Barney's — 'Croppies Lie Down' — but now in her tension she couldn't remember the words.

'In fact I want you to do nothing. That's the way I like it.'

'Could I have the money?'

'Yes, yes.' He was impatient now and fumbled with the wallet, then saw the money on the desk. The roll of notes made a comfortable bulge in the hip pocket of her jeans. He locked the door as she lay on the bed. It was like being asked to lie on a doctor's couch. Mr Henderson knelt and patted and prodded her to his liking. No sooner was she settled than he said,

'Perhaps you'd better take your clothes off.'

She had to get up again. There was a hole in her pants stretched to an egg shape just below her navel. She turned her back on him then, when undressed, lay down, her body all knuckles.

His eyes widened and went heavy. He couldn't decide whether to take off his glasses or leave them on. He began to talk baby-talk, to speak to her as if she wasn't there. He told her how he had ached after her slim undernourished body for months, how he had watched her from between the banisters, how he loved to see her on her hands and knees and the triangle of light that he could always see between her thighs when she wore her jeans. He was fascinated by her bruises and kissed each one of them lightly. Spoke to her bruises. She was sweating a nervous sweat from her armpits. Praised her thinness, her each rib, the tent bones of her hips and her tuft

of hair between. He smelt all over her as she had seen dogs do,
but by now she had closed her eyes and could only feel the
touch of his breath, his nosings. It went on for ages. Her fists
were clenched. She tried to remember her shopping list. A
pan loaf, maybe some small bread – sodas. Sugar – she needed
sugar and potatoes and tea-bags and mince and cornflakes.
Mr Henderson climbed on to the bed, having opened her
legs, but succeeded only in delivering himself somewhere in
the coverlet with a groan. She looked down at him. His hair
was still damp and moistening her belly. His face was hidden
from her. The back of his neck was red and criss-crossed with
wrinkles. Beneath the window she could hear her baby crying
and farther away the sound of a blackbird.

When he got his breath back he went to the bathroom. Liz
dressed in a hurry and went downstairs, trying to master the
shudders that went through her like nausea. She inserted the
dummy in the baby's mouth, grabbed Paul from the playroom and fled the house, drawing the pram after her against
the gravel.

The kiosk outside the Co-op smelt of piss, would have
smelt worse if it had not been for the ventilation of the broken
panes. A taxi arrived within minutes and she coaxed the
driver to collapse the pram and put it in the boot.

'In the name of God, Missus, how does this thing operate?'

In a traffic jam – there must have been a bomb scare
somewhere – she fed the baby milk from a cold bottle.

Her mother lived at the other side of town and was
surprised to see her drawing up in such style. Liz told the
driver to wait and hurried her mother into accepting the story
that a friend's husband had run off with another woman and
the girl was in a terrible state and she, Liz, was going to spend
the night with her, and Mammy would you mind the kids?
Her mother was old but not yet helpless and had raised six of
her own. At twenty-two Liz was the last and felt she could
call on her for special favours. She gave her a fiver to get

herself some wee thing. A tenner, she thought, would have brought questions in its wake.

'You're a pet,' she called to her, rushing from the door.

Coming from Marks and Spencer's, she walked past the Methodist Church in Donegal Place. An old man was changing the black notice-board which kept up with the death toll of the troubles. She hesitated and watched him. He had removed a 5 from 1875 and was fumbling and clacking with the wooden squares which slotted in like a hymn board. He was exasperatingly slow and she walked on but could not resist looking back over her shoulder.

Going through security, the woman stirred her jeans and jumper tentatively at the bottom of her carrier bag. The hotel lobby was crowded with newsmen with bandoliers of cameras, talking in groups. She asked the price of bed and breakfast and found that she had more than enough. Would she be having dinner? Liz leaned forward to the clerk.

'How much?'

The clerk smiled and said anything from five to fifty pounds. Liz thought a moment and said yes. She wanted to pay there and then but the clerk insisted that she could settle her bill in the morning.

'Elizabeth O'Prey' she signed on the register card, taking great care to make it neat. At school she had never been much good but everybody praised her handwriting; teachers said she had a gift for it. She had been Elizabeth Wilson and one of the few advantages of her marriage, she thought, had been the opportunity of a flourishing Y at the end of O'Prey. As she had signed for her family allowance and sickness benefit she had perfected it.

She tried not to stare at the magnificence of the place, the plush maroon carpet, the glittering lights, the immaculately uniformed staff. She felt nervous about doing or saying the wrong thing. She didn't have a posh accent like those around her and rather than put it on she said as few words as possible. She was conscious of people looking at her and was glad that she had changed in the shop. As the desk clerk answered the phone she saw herself in a mirrored alcove, new shoes, hair done, new peach-coloured summer dress, and was happily surprised. For a second she didn't look like herself. Her Marks and Spencer's polythene bag was the only thing that jarred. She should have bought a real bag.

'Excuse me, madam,' said the clerk, clamping the earpiece against her shoulder, 'would you mind if security checked you out again?'

'They already searched me.'

'If you wouldn't mind.'

A woman in uniform came out and showed Liz to a small room. She was stout with blonde curly hair bursting from beneath her peaked cap, chewing-gum in a mouth heavy with lip-gloss. Her body seemed pumped into the uniform. She searched Liz's carrier bag thoroughly.

'Why are you searching me twice?'

'You have a Belfast address, you have no luggage.' She came towards Liz, who raised her arms obediently. 'Why are you staying here?' Her heavy hands moved over Liz's small breasts, beneath her arms to her waist, down her buttocks and thighs. She had never been searched as thoroughly as this before — a series of light touches was all she'd had. This woman was groping her as if she expected to find something beneath her skin.

'My husband put me out,' said Liz. A forefinger scored up the track between her buttocks and she jumped.

'That's all right, love. We have to be sure.' She smiled, handing her back her carrier bag. 'I hope you and your man get it sorted out.'

A bell-boy who was twice her age turned his back to her in the quiet of the lift before he showed her to her room. He made no attempt to carry her polythene bag.

When she closed and locked the door she felt for the first time in years that she was alone. She could not believe it. She stood with her back to the door, her hands behind her resting on the handle. The room took her breath away. Matching curtains and bedspread of tangerine flowers with one corner of the sheets folded back to show that they too matched. She walked around the room touching things lightly. From her window she could see a wedge of red-brick Belfast vibrating in the heat. This height above the street she could hear no sound. She lay on the bed, trying it for size and comfort, and to her disappointment it creaked slightly. The bathroom was done in rust shades with carpet going up the outside of the bath.

The first thing she had decided to do was to have a shower. Her new dress did nothing to remove the crawling sensation on her skin when she thought of Mr Henderson. Before undressing she turned on the test card on the television just for a bit of sound. She had never had a shower before and it took her ages to get it to work, then even longer to get the temperature right, but when she did get in she felt like a film star. Her instinct was to save the hot water but she remembered where she was and how much she was paying. She must have stayed in the shower for twenty minutes soaping and resoaping herself, watching the drapes of suds sliding down her body and away. The bruises remained.

She put on the new underwear and felt luxuriant to be padding about free in her bra and pants. Although the shower was good she decided that before she went to bed she would have a bath so hot the steam would mist the mirrors. She would buy some magazines and smoke and read, propped up by all those pillows. Watch television *from* bed, maybe.

In the bar she felt good, for the first time in years felt herself. She sat at a stool at the counter and sipped a vodka and orange. The bar was loud with groups of people talking. She caught herself staring in the bar mirror as she looked

around. A man came in and sat next to her on a free stool. She
wondered if he was waiting for someone. He ordered a drink,
asked her to pass the water jug for his whisky. She smiled. He
slowly tilted the jug until it was upright and obviously
empty and then they both laughed. He asked the barmaid for
water.

'Are you American?' Liz asked. He nodded. He looked a
good deal older than her, in his mid-thirties or forty, she
guessed, with a plain face and a blond moustache. He had bad
skin, pock-marked, but it gave him a rugged look. She
imagined him on horseback.

'Yeah, and you?'

'Oh, I'm from here.'

'There's no need to apologise.' He laughed and poured
water into his whisky slowly. She watched it mix in wreaths
with the spirit. He tasted the drink and seemed satisfied. She
became alone again as she bought herself cigarettes and
matches. They drank separately in the noise. She crumpled
the silver paper, dropped it in the ash-tray and offered him
one. He refused with a spread hand. He asked the barmaid for
a menu, which he studied.

'Are you gonna eat?' he asked. She nodded, with her
mouth full of vodka and orange. 'It's quite good here. I can
recommend their *coq au vin*.'

'Are you staying here?' He nodded. She asked him if he was
on holiday and he said that he was working, a journalist of
sorts.

'Oh, how interesting.' When she had said it she could have
bitten her tongue out, it sounded so phoney. She heard
Eamonn mimicking and repeating her tones, but this man
did not seem to notice. She asked,

'What paper?'

The piece he would do would be syndicated. She nodded
and took another sip of her drink. There was a pause as he
studied the menu.

'Excuse my iggerence,' said Liz, 'but what does that mean
— sin . . . sin . . . ?'

'Sorry. It just means that the same story goes in lots of
papers — and I get more money.'

Liz tap-tapped her cigarette with her index finger over the
ash-tray but it was not smoked enough for any of it to fall.

'You say you're from here,' he said. 'If you don't mind me
asking, which side are you on?'

'I'm sort of in the middle.'

'That can't help.'

'Well I was born nothing — but a Protestant nothing and I
married a Catholic nothing and so I'm now a mixture of
nothing. I hate the whole thing. I couldn't give a damn.'

'One of the silent minority.' He smiled. 'Boy, have you got
problems.' Liz thought he was talking about her.

'Me?'

'Not you — the country.'

They talked for a while and went separately in to dinner.
When he saw that she too was eating at a table on her own he
came over and suggested that they eat together. She agreed,
grateful for someone to help her with choosing from the
menu. Rather than attempt to say the dishes, she pointed and
he ordered. The array of knives and forks frightened her but
she did what he did, American style, cutting up and eating
with the fork alone. He told her that he had been a Catholic
priest and that he had left when he had had a crisis of
conscience, Vietnam, contraception, the nature of authority
all contributing. As a priest he had written a weekly column
for a Catholic paper in Boston, and when he left the Church to
continue working in journalism was natural. He admitted to
being married shortly after being laicised. She said she too
was married.

He made her feel good, relaxed. In his company she felt she
could say anything. After telling of himself he asked her
questions about her life. The questions he asked no one had

ever asked her before and she had to think hard to answer them. In her replies she got mixed up, found she was contradicting herself, but got out of it by laughing.

'This is like an interview on the T.V.,' she said and he apologised but went on asking her questions, about her life, about the way she felt and thought. His eyes were blue and gentle, widening at some of the things she said. Except for his pitted skin she found him attractive. He listened with the slightest inclination of the head, looking up at her almost. Being from America he probably didn't know about her accent. Maybe she looked high-class in her peach rig-out. Liz spoke until she realised she was speaking, then she became self-conscious.

'I hope you're not taking all this down,' she said laughing.

'No, but it sure helps to talk to someone like you — a nothing as you so nicely put it. It helps the balance.'

Hesitatingly she told him something of her relationship, or lack of it, with Eamonn. 'You have your troubles,' was all he would say.

When they had finished eating he suggested that they go through to the bar to have a liqueur. He was behind her, easing her seat away from the table before she realised it and he was equally attentive and concerned holding the bar door open for her.

'You're a gentleman,' she said.

'My old man used to say that a gentleman was someone who made a woman feel like a lady.'

He introduced her to Bailey's Irish Cream.

'It's gorgeous,' she said, 'like sweets. You could drink that all night.'

'You could not,' he said, smiling.

Liz settled back in the seat and lit a cigarette. She slapped her stomach lightly.

'God, I'm full,' she said, 'and I feel great. I haven't felt like this for ages.'

They had another Bailey's Irish Cream, which she insisted on buying. Then when he had finished it he said, slapping his knees,

'I must go. I have some work to finish for tomorrow. Will you excuse me?'

'Sure.' She tried to make it sound as if she was not disappointed at all but was conscious that some of his accent was invading her speech. She detained him a little longer, asking him to wait till she finished another cigarette but eventually he said he must go up to his room.

'I don't want to sit here on my owney-o,' said Liz. 'I think I'll just go up too.'

In the lift there was a silence between them. Liz felt she had to talk.

'What floor are you on?'

'I pressed number four and you're on six.'

'That's right.'

She told him her room number and then thought it too forward. She hadn't meant to tell him but the silence of the humming lift forced her to say it.

Getting out of the lift, he touched her arm with his hand, then shook hands.

'It's been a real pleasure meeting you,' he said. The lift doors nipped her view of his smile as he waved goodbye.

In her room the aloneness changed from what she had felt earlier. Now it seemed enforced. She wanted to go on talking. In the mirror she shrugged, made a face and laughed at herself. The only thing to read was a Bible on the bedside table and she was annoyed that she had forgotten to buy some magazines. She had the hot bath she had promised herself, but afterwards was too warm so she opened a window on to the distant sound of the street.

She prodded the buttons on the television set and for want of anything better settled on 'Call My Bluff' with that nice man with the pink bow tie and the moustache. In her new underwear she sat propped up on tangerine pillows, smoking – viewing in style. Where did they get the words from? Clinchpoop? Liz guessed it was the thing the man said about the plague but it turned out to be somebody who didn't know what to do – like eating peas with your knife or backslapping at a funeral. That was her, she thought. She never knew what to do at the time. Later on she knew what she should and could have done. And it was not just with manners. She had no control over the direction of her life. She was far too bloody soft. From now on she should lock Eamonn out and begin to fight her own corner – for the children's sake at least.

She jumped out of bed and pressed the channel buttons. After the ads it was part three of something so she switched off. The room was very quiet. She got back into bed again, hearing its annoying creak and the crispness of its sheets.

She should have told that Henderson to get knotted. It was the end of her job – there was no way she could go back there again. He would hang about like a dog every morning from now on pointing at her with his trousers. Resignation. That was all that was left to her. But then Eamonn would want to know why she had quit. Tell him Henderson had made a pass at her – which was true. Maybe he'd want to know where she'd spent the night. She had run to her mother's before because of a fight. If he noticed she'd been away at all. The peach dress she would have to leave in the wardrobe. Or she could leave it at her mother's until she found an excuse to bring it home. Why hadn't she thought of it before? She could pass it off as good jumble sale stuff.

Pleased with herself, she lay down among the pillows and spread her feet warm and wide. With the lamp out, car headlights swung yellow wedges across the ceiling. The net curtains ballooned slowly and fell back again. She thought of her baby sleeping in the spare bed at her mother's, walled in by pillows, and Paul, open-mouthed in sleep, snuggling in to his Gran. 'That child has knees on him like knuckles,' the old woman had once complained. Liz spread her opened fingers across the sheets, trying to take up as much room as possible in the bed. She smelt the strange perfumed hotel soap off her own body, felt the summer night warmth on her face and tried, as she drifted off to sleep, to forget the fact that Eamonn, for the loss of her weekly wage, would kill her when he got her home — if not before.

No Joke

O N THE MORNING of his eighty-third birthday Frank Stringer awoke and felt the oink encrusted in the corners of his eyes again. He knuckled them clean.

'Callisthenics,' he said and swung his feet out of bed. He began a series of bends and stretches which he had performed each morning for the past twenty years, except for a period when his ankle was mending after falling down the steps of his local pub. During this period he did the arm exercises sitting up in bed.

Breathless and panting through his nose, he made his way to the bathroom. He lathered his face and addressed the mirror. His bushy hair matched the whiteness of the soap on his chin. He cut pink swathes in it with great satisfaction.

'Angry employer,' he said. 'Jones, you should have been here at nine o'clock.' He changed the tone of his voice to a piping treble, 'Why, sir, what happened?' His shoulders began to shake up and down but the sight of himself laughing in the mirror always brought it to a stop. It was the same with crying. When he had finished shaving he twisted the handle of the razor and watched its butterfly wings open. He removed the stainless steel blade, washed it clean and left it to drain dry on the tiled sill. He walked along the landing and knocked on the other two doors.

'Good morning all,' he shouted. 'Time to get up.' Then he

made his way down the stairs and put the kettle on. He put two slices of white bread under the grill, and switched on the transistor just in time to hear the pips. He stopped and stared for a while at the darkness outside. The rain on the window made haloes round the street lamps. He tried to remember what classes he had that day.

The kitchen door opened and Violet came pouncing in.

'Do you know what time . . . Jesus,' she squealed and dived to the grill-pan which was issuing clouds of blue smoke. She carried the grill-pan with its two black and flaming bits of bread to the back door and slung them out into the dark garden.

'Do you know the time, Daddy? It's seven o'clock.'

'I must have looked at the clock wrongly. I *am* sorry.'

'You'll be up early the morning of your funeral,' Violet scowled. Her face was puffy with sleep and she wore a lemon dressing-gown that made her look jaundiced.

'It's not the end of the world,' said the old man. After a moment he said, 'Has the post arrived yet?'

'Daddy, it's five past seven. The postman comes at eight.' There was grapefruit in her voice. 'Why? Are you expecting . . .' She broke off and came across to him, put her arm over his shoulders from behind.

'I'm sorry, love, I forgot. It's your birthday. Happy birthday.' She bent over and gave him a kiss on the cheek.

'You're right. I'd forgotten. Watch the toast.'

Heather came in, prepared as always, and gave her father an envelope and a small parcel. She was the younger of the two, not yet fifty, and she had always indulged her father.

'Happy birthday, Daddy,' she said. He opened the wrapping and found a tie-pin and a tie. He admired them out loud.

'Who are they from?' he asked, looking up.

'From me,' said Heather.

'Do you know the time, Heather?' said Violet.

'Yes, Vi, he's done it again.'

As they ate breakfast the old man said,

'Did you hear about the unfunny egg?'

'Yes, but tell us again,' said Violet.

'No yolk.' His hand shook as he laughed, wobbling the tea perilously close to the rim of the cup. His daughters chewed and looked at each other. Violet said, then shouted, at her father,

'SO YOU'RE HAVING A PARTY this afternoon?'

'What?' he said. 'There's no need to shout. I'm not deaf.'

'Well, are you?'

'Deaf?'

'No, having a party?'

'Yes, the fools.' He laughed and clomped his false teeth. 'A little celebration for my birthday. I got them to agree to it.'

Heather began to clear the breakfast things. She said over her shoulder,

'How are we supposed to pass the time from now until eight-thirty?'

'I've some jotters to correct,' said Vi.

'I suppose I could do some of my own. What a depressing way to start the day.'

The old man hadn't got rid of whatever was annoying him so he took his teeth out and washed them under the tap.

'Daddy, must you?'

'What?'

'Wash your dentures in the dishwater?'

'Oh, stuff and nonsense.'

He shuffled into the dining room and waited until he heard the girls go up to dress. Then he opened the drinks cupboard and lifted out an unlabelled green bottle. From his inside breast pocket he produced a silver hip-flask and began to fill it. He was inordinately proud that there wasn't the slightest shake in his hand for his age and the wiping of the outside of the flask was merely a reflex action. He slipped it back into his wallet pocket.

'To warm the heart,' he said, patting it.

He sat in his armchair, his fingertips joined, watching the dawn and trying to remember a poem of Baudelaire's. He tried to remember it until Heather came in dressed and heavy with make-up, looking for her handbag.

'Is it the ambulance or the taxi to call for you this morning?'

'The ambulance.'

In the black taxi Frank Stringer sat straight-backed with his feet together and the window rolled down. When the others got in they complained of the draught and he allowed them to close it.

'Myself, I was born in a field,' he said, 'and I have drunk whisky from a damp cup without the slightest ill-effect.'

Their taxi was the first to arrive at the Day Centre and as usual Frank got out to help the others from the relatively high step on to the pavement. It was good to be first because the tea was freshly made. He was also glad to see that his ordered copy of *Le Canard* had arrived, even though it was two days late. He sat reading his paper – some years ago he had conceded to wearing glasses for newsprint – and sipping his tea, not joining in the conversation. All they seemed to talk about was their ailments and how they had slept and he preferred at this early hour to withdraw behind his paper.

Gradually the place began to fill up. There was that strange woman who smelt of, and ate, caraway seed. And Mr and Mrs Hill doubly bent double. They were the most decrepit pair, leaning on walking sticks held with shining knuckles almost at the level of their stooped heads. For Stringer they were the ultimate in age. With laughing scorn the worst he could say of any new arrival to the Day Centre was that they were 'as old as the Hills'. There was voluminous

Bella, whose lisle stocking-tops occasionally hung down like the tops of fishing waders, and Maud, all covered with cameos, her pneumatic fingers glittering with rings which would never again come off – every time the phone rang distantly in the office she assumed it would be for her – and Agnes Crookshanks, her face tilted by a stroke, who thought she owned a labrador. It was odd, Frank thought, how women carried their age worse than men. Somewhere a bell rang.

'Well, I'm off to class,' he said. He left the staff room and walked the corridor to Room 23. It was empty, so he sat down to wait for them. There must have been some hold-up at registration.

Gradually the others began to filter into the Day Room and Sister Herd, who was in charge, got them started on their activities. She wished Stringer a happy birthday and joked with him about the riotous time they were going to have at his party. She was full of winks and nods and comforting pats. When Stringer was sitting down she would even permit him to put his arm around her hips as they talked. He could pretend to be a daftie when it suited him. Picasso had fathered a child when he was eighty-one, but he doubted whether Sister Herd, despite all her friendliness, would submit herself to the test.

Stringer began to get his materials together. Nurse O'Neil came forward, stepping slowly, one step at a time, her hands joined as if she would break into an aria, leading an old man who was slowly lifting and setting down his aluminium walking aid. After a long time they drew level with where Stringer sat.

'Good morning, Mr Stringer,' said the nurse, 'here's a little friend for you.' She introduced Mr Scott, but the new man would not risk letting go of his walking aid long enough to shake hands. He ignored Stringer's outstretched hand.

'You'll show him what we do here, won't you, Mr Stringer? I'll leave him in your care.'

Stringer jumped to his feet and got Mr Scott settled in a chair.

'Now then,' he said, sitting down beside him, 'what we are engaged in here is the making of crackers.' He indicated the different coloured piles of crepe paper, the stickers, the caps for the bang and finally the box of jokes and plastic trinkets which had to be put into each. He demonstrated for him the process, at what stage to insert the joke and trinket, and the little machine that crimped and rolled the paper and produced a perfect Christmas cracker. Finally he unfurled his tongue and gave a cow's lick to a label of a Christmas tree and stuck it on the barrel of the cracker.

'Do you follow me so far?'

Mr Scott shook his head to say that he did not. But, Stringer noticed, Mr Scott was palsied and always shook his head as if saying no.

'Is that clear?'

'Yes,' said Mr Scott, shaking his head from side to side. He began to attempt the process of making a cracker, looking up at Stringer every so often.

'What did she say your name was?'

'Stringer. Frank Stringer.'

'I thought so.'

'Are you an educated man, Mr Scott?'

'Reasonably so. You ought to know.'

'How should I know? Your accent tells me something, but I have known many dunderheads with cut-glass voices.'

'You taught me.'

'I *did*?'

Stringer stared at him. Mr Scott was bald, had a small white moustache and a face like a tomato under pressure. He did not look like a pupil.

'Yes, a long time ago,' said Mr Scott, 'at St Thomas of Aquin's.'

'Yes, that's right. Scott? Scott? It's all gone now.' He

looked at the man's face, hoping for a spark of recognition but could find none. 'What are you working at these days?'

'I'm retired – from the Law.' Mr Scott seemed glum about it.

'Ah, you'll have to forgive me. I tend to wander a little – so they tell me.' Stringer pulled his chair closer to Scott's. 'This is very interesting. I have so many questions to ask. Did you ever keep up your French?'

'No. Except for a bit during the war, holidays – that kind of thing.'

'I was just this morning sitting trying to remember a poem of Baudelaire's.'

'Which one?'

'Any one.' Frank Stringer tapped the side of his head. 'Things are getting a little difficult in here.' Mr Scott nodded sympathetically. 'Do you remember anything I taught you?'

'No.'

'Do you remember anything I ever said?'

Mr Scott hesitated. 'No,' he said, 'wait . . . there was one thing.'

'What?'

'Something you said all the time – a kind of catch-phrase. I'll never forget it.'

'What was it?'

'How did it go now . . . oh yes, "Boys, boys. Is there a life before death? That's what I want to know." '

'I never said that.'

'Yes you did.'

'That was Egan's phrase.'

'Who?'

'Egan, the Latin master,' said Stringer. 'At least I think that's what his name was.'

'I don't remember any Egan. Was he Bald Eagle?'

'Bald Eagle? Why did you call him that?'

'Because he was bald.'

'If my memory serves me correctly he was thin on top. Yes, that was his phrase. He used it in the staff room too. It's certainly not a sentiment I would associate myself with. "Is there a life before death",' he said scornfully.

They continued to make crackers as they talked, Stringer pausing only to lick the final stickers.

'I am, as they say nowadays, *into* living. Because I don't believe in God I'm not afraid to die and because I'm not afraid of death I enjoy my life. It's just *because* it's so transient . . .' He held up his hand like a Shakespearian actor of the old school and declaimed. 'The thought of death produces a precious and fragrant drop of levity which invigorates the whole of my life.'

'You're a piss artist, if you ask me,' said Mr Scott.

'The sole drive of Christianity, of all religion, is to answer the problem of death. I say there isn't a problem. Forget it. Be happy. "Death, thou shalt die." '

'I think I've rolled this one back to front,' said Mr Scott.

Stringer examined the cracker and said,

'Perfectly acceptable.' He fed it into the machine.

Sister Herd came into the room again and suggested that they keep today's batch of crackers aside for the party that afternoon.

'Good thinking, Sister,' said Stringer, reaching out his arm to encircle her neat bottom but she took a little skip-step past him to the raffia table.

For the party Frank had requested that they be allowed to bring in a few beers but Sister Herd had flatly refused. It was to begin at two o'clock and everything had to be cleared by three. The kitchen staff had baked a huge cake but either the budget or the surface area of icing couldn't hold eighty-three candles. Instead they compromised and used eight red ones, which Sister Herd said represented tens, and three blue ones which represented units. Frank blew them out and everyone sang 'Happy Birthday'. All his life he had hated the way his name hadn't fitted into that tune and had to be broken into two syllables where only one existed,

> Happy Birthday, dear Fra – ank,
> Happy Birthday to you.

What was even worse was when they used 'Frankie' to make it scan.

Then they all pulled crackers and read the jokes to each other with perplexed faces and put on paper hats and blew things which unfurled with a squeak. A wavering voice asked if there was any caraway seed in the cake.

'Mr Scott, could I have a word in your shell-like ear?' said Stringer. Mr Scott leaned over to listen. 'Have you been known to take strong drink?' Looking at his complexion Frank knew the answer and ignored the palsied nodding.

'Well, if we could adjourn to the quiet haven of the corner I have a little something for us.'

Frank asked for two teas without milk. Mr Scott, setting down and picking up his aluminium frame, slowly moved to the corner. Frank followed him, carrying the two cups. He looked around, then quickly tipped the steaming tea into the soil of a large cheese plant. He looked at it, expecting it to wither almost at once.

'This tree is a bit like my mind,' he said ' – full of holes.'

As he spoke he reached into his pocket and poured two substantial drams into the cups, shielding the flask from the nurses with his body.

'This, I may tell you, is the best of stuff. The best single malt in the world – from the island of Islay. From Laphroaig. One hundred and ten proof. Untouched by human foot.' Seeing Scott's mouth open for a question Stringer said, 'A friend. I am willing to go no further than that.'

They sat down and inhaled the vapour. Mr Scott looked apprehensive.

'Drink it quickly,' said Stringer, 'before they smell it.' They downed their cups of tea in one.

'Taste the peat?' asked Stringer after a long pause.

'The peat's on fire,' Scott tried to say but couldn't make himself understood. They made joint noises of suffering and satisfaction.

'I must say, Scottie, it's a sad reflection on education that you don't remember a single thing I taught you.'

'I remember one thing about you.'

'Not that "life before death" thing.'

'No.'

'What, then?'

'In my first year at Aquin's you caned me until I cried.'

There was a silence between them. Then Stringer said, 'What for?'

'The thing is I can't rightly remember. All I know is I got six, three across the fingertips of each hand. I wept. It was the only time in my school career that I was beaten. I'll never forget it.'

'I wonder what it was for? I'm sure you deserved it,' Stringer laughed.

'I know I didn't.' Scott did not join in his laughter.

'I must have been straight out of college at the time. Later I learned to discipline classes without the cane.'

'I wasn't a class.'

They both sat staring into their empty cups. Stringer said, 'I eventually became Head. When were you at Aquin's?'

After a moment's thought Scott told him his years and they coincided with Stringer's early years as a teacher.

'Here, have another dram,' Stringer said, getting up to shield the flask as he poured, 'and let bygones be bygones.'

'I became a magistrate. I think I was always fair and lenient. So, perversely, you probably taught me something.'

'Thank you very much.'

'What was Archie's second name?'

'Archie who?'

'The Headmaster during our time.'

'Gillfillan? What about him?'

'I complained about you to him. That I had been beaten unfairly.'

'It was that important to you? What did he say?'

'He laughed and gave me a jujube from a paper bag he kept in the drawer of his desk. He told me I should be in class.'

'The jujubes,' Stringer laughed, remembering.

'Did he ever mention my complaint?'

'He may have done. I can't remember that far back.' He turned to Scott and looked him straight in the eyes. 'I was inexperienced, Scott.'

Mr Scott looked away from him at the leather-green leaves of the cheese plant.

'You must have been a lily-livered boy to take it so badly.'

There was another silence between them which lasted for a long time.

'Mr Scott, you have succeeded in depressing me on my birthday.'

They drank simultaneously and again made smacking, pained noises and sat staring in front of them.

Someone had put on a record player and a few couples were dancing on the lino-tiled floor. The Hills had straightened up as much as they could and formed a slow-moving human archway. After one dance Bella's stocking-tops hung down beneath her dress. Sister Herd was trying to coax the more active ones on to the floor. She was moving about trying to organise, acting the hostess. Stringer said,

'Did you know, Mr Scott, that the Romans drank the health of their hostess as many times as there were letters in her name? Herd is easy. What would happen to us if she was something like Bartholomew-Merryweather, eh?' He laughed with his head thrown back.

'I don't know what you're talking about.'

Sister Herd came across to them.

'Well, Mr Scott, is he looking after you?' Mr Scott nodded.

'Mr Stringer, pull this cracker with me. I think it's the last.' She tugged the cracker against Stringer's resistance and it went *phhht*!

'Not with a bang but a whimper,' Stringer said. He had won the larger share and looked inside it.

'No joke,' he said. 'Someone has not been doing their work properly – *and* no trinket.' His voice had risen to the pitch of a teacher confronting his class. Mr Scott looked sheepishly at the floor as Sister Herd went off to entertain someone else.

'This will not do, Scott. Not in my section. I would never stand for slovenly workmanship and I'm not going to start now.' Scott couldn't tell whether he was serious or not.

'You assume that it was me and not yourself who made the mistake.'

'Of course. This is your first day.'

'You have already told me that you have a head like a cheese plant. Might it not have been you who forgot to put in the joke?'

'Certainly not.' Stringer groaned and put both his hands on his knees. 'I will continue this investigation in a moment. Right now, Nature calls.' He stood up and swayed so badly that he had to grip on to the table top to stop himself falling. He fell back into his chair for safety.

'I seem to have misjudged, if you'll pardon the expression,' he said. 'Lend me your thing, Scottie. I need to go to the lavatory.'

For the first time that day Mr Scott laughed.

'Use your own thing,' he said. Stringer stood up again and

pulled Scott's aluminium walking aid from him. He started to laugh.

'I'm distinctly pissed,' he said and began to hobble towards the lavatory, moving the frame in front of him. He shouted over his shoulder, 'As a matter of fact I'm as pissed as a fart.'

Mr Scott tried to shhh him.

In the lavatory Stringer knew he had taken too much too quickly. He had to lean his forehead against the cool tiles above the urinal to steady himself. His flies caused him some difficulty because he was laughing so much. Somehow he got back to his seat.

'Are you a believer, Mr Scott?' he asked, falling down into the chair.

'In some things.'

'What a stupid thing to say. Do you believe in God?'

'Yes.'

'I thought as much. God is a joke.' Suddenly his eyes lit up. 'It's like our cracker just now. It'll be like that on the Day of Judgment. *Phht*! He's a joke and he's not there. Believe me, we're far better off without him.'

'But you taught in a Catholic school,' said Scott.

'What better reason for not believing in God any more? It's as plain as a pikestaff. Why should God be a creative artist? Why does everything in religion fit like a poem? Because it *is* a poem. That's all. The prophecies all come true. Bethlehem means the City of Bread, where Christ was born. He became flesh, he became bread. The miracle of the *loaves* and fishes. Christ's symbol was a fish. His Crucifixion at the Passover. It's all too neat. Here, have another dram. It's good stuff.'

'Not for me, please, my head is going round.'

Frank poured himself another and let it stay in the cup for a while. It was the colour of weak tea.

It was now five past three and some taxi-men were beginning to hover around inside the doors. As he drank off the whisky, Frank became aware of the applause and a chant went up for a speech from the birthday boy.

'Speech! Speech! Come on, Frank, a few words.'

Stringer heaved himself to his feet and leaned on Scott's aluminium frame like a dais. The crowd quietened. There was absolute silence, which he commanded with his eyes. He cleared his throat.

'I would just like to take this opportunity to say thank you to one and all for your presence here today. Especially I would like to thank the lovely Sister Herd for her untiring zeal in helping to organise our little party . . . '

There was a spatter of uncertain applause. He politely waited for it to die down. He felt himself sway back and tightened his grip on the aluminium frame but it was so light it came up with him. He swayed forward again and managed to set it down.

'Above all I would like to thank His Lordship the Bishop for sparing the time out of a very busy schedule to attend and distribute the prizes . . . '

There was some tittering from the back of the hall but he quelled it with a look. He went on.

'I want to take this opportunity to remind parents that, except for a small number of pupils excused on medical grounds, all pupils are required to take Physical Education at school and should, therefore, be provided with a P.E. kit comprising of . . . '

Sister Herd came forward and put her hand on his elbow.

'We're running late,' she whispered. He paused and in the silence Sister Herd spoke loudly, thanking everyone, especially the kitchen staff and Mr Stringer himself, and announced that the ambulances and taxis were waiting at the door, and that they should all sing 'Happy Birthday' for the last time.

They all sang the song and still he hated 'dear Fra – ank'. Sister Herd detached his hands from Mr Scott's frame and, gripping his unsteadiness tightly by the elbow, led him towards the doors. Mr Scott followed at a pace considerably slower than his usual.

'That was a lovely speech, Mr Stringer,' said Sister Herd.

'That bastard of a Bishop had it coming to him.'

'Yes indeed, you spoke out for all of us.'

In the taxi on the last leg of the journey he cried a little but seeing himself reflected in the glass partition he stopped. The taxi-driver had to manhandle him into the house. Once inside he fell into a comatose sleep on the sofa and when he awoke his two daughters, in rollers and dressing-gowns, were correcting jotters amidst the débris of the tea table.

The Beginnings of a Sin

I BELIEVE HE'S LATE again thought Colum. He took a clean white surplice from his bag and slipped it over his head, steadying his glasses as he did so. It was five to eight. He sat on the bench and changed his shoes for a black pair of gutties. Father Lynch said that all his altar-boys must move as quietly as shadows. When he was late he was usually in his worst mood. Sometimes he did not turn up at all and Miss Grant, the housekeeper, would come over and announce from the back of the church that Father Lynch was ill and that there would be no Mass that day.

At two minutes to eight Colum heard his footstep at the vestry door. Father Lynch came in and nodded to the boy. Colum had never seen anyone with such a sleep-crumpled face in the mornings. It reminded him of a bloodhound, there was such a floppiness about his deeply wrinkled skin. His whole face sagged and sloped into lines of sadness. His black hair was parted low to the side and combed flat with Brylcreem. Colum thought his neat hair looked out of place on top of the disorder of his features.

'Is everything ready?' Father Lynch asked him.

'Yes, Father.'

Colum watched him as he prepared to say Mass. He began by putting on the amice, like a handkerchief with strings, at the back of his neck. Next a white alb like a shroud, reaching

135

to the floor. The polished toe-caps of his everyday shoes peeped out from underneath. He put the cincture about his waist and knotted it quickly. He kissed the embroidered cross on his emerald stole and hung it round his neck. Lastly he put on the chasuble, very carefully inserting his head through the neck-hole. Colum couldn't make up his mind whether he did not want to stain the vestments with hair-oil or wreck his hair. The chasuble was emerald green with yellow lines. Colum liked the feasts of the martyrs best, with their bright blood colour. Father Lynch turned to him.

'What are you staring at?'

'Nothing, Father.'

'You look like a wee owl.'

'Sorry.'

'Let's get this show on the road,' Father Lynch said, his face still like a sad bloodhound. 'We're late already.'

None of the other altar-boys liked Father Lynch. When they did something wrong, he never scolded them with words but instead would nip them on the upper arm. They said he was too quiet and you could never trust anybody like that. Colum found that he was not so quiet if you asked him questions. He seemed to like Colum better than the others, at least Colum thought so. One day he had asked him why a priest wore so much to say Mass and Father Lynch had spoken to him for about ten minutes, keeping him late for school.

'Normally when people wear beautiful things it is to make their personality stand out. With a priest it is the opposite. He wears so much to hide himself. And the higher up the Church you go, the more you have to wear. Think of the poor Pope with all that trumphery on him.'

After Mass Father Lynch asked him how the ballot tickets were going.

'Great. I've sold —'

'Don't tell me. Keep it as a surprise.'

In the darkness Colum stood at the door waiting. He had rolled up a white ballot ticket and was smoking it, watching his breath cloud the icy air. He pulled his socks up as high as he could to try and keep his legs warm. There was a funny smell from the house, like sour food. The woman came back out with her purse. She was still chewing something.

'What's it in aid of?'

'St Kieran's Church Building Fund.'

'How much are they?'

'Threepence each.'

The woman hesitated, poking about in her purse with her index finger. He told her that the big prize was a Christmas hamper. There was a second prize of whiskey and sherry. She took four tickets, finishing his last book.

'Father Lynch'll not be wanting to win it outright, then.'

He was writing her name on the stubs with his fountain pen.

'Pardon?'

'You're a neat wee writer,' she said. He tore the tickets down the perforations and gave them to her. She handed him a shilling, which he dropped into his jacket pocket. It was swinging heavy with coins.

'There's the snow coming on now,' said the woman, waiting to close the front door. He ran the whole way home holding on to the outside of his pocket. In the house he dried his hair and wiped the speckles of melted snow from his glasses. Two of his older brothers, Rory and Dermot, were sitting on the sofa doing homework balanced on their knees and when he told them it was snowing they ran out to see if it was lying.

He took down his tin and spilled it and the money from his pocket on to the table. He added it all together and counted the number of books of stubs. For each book sold the seller was allowed to keep sixpence for himself. Over the past weeks Colum had sold forty-two books around the doors. He took a pound note and a shilling and slipped them into his pocket. He had never had so much money in his life and there was still a full week to sell tickets before the ballot was drawn.

His mother stood at the range making soda farls on a griddle. When they were cooked they filled the house with their smell and made a dry scuffling noise as she handled them. He heard the front door close and Michael shout 'Hello'. At eighteen he was the eldest and the only wage earner in the house.

'Come on, Colum,' said his mother. 'Clear that table. The hungry working man is in.'

After tea they always said the Family Rosary. Colum would half kneel, half crouch at the armchair with his face almost touching the seat. The cushion smelt of cloth and human. He tried to say the Rosary as best he could, thinking of the Sacred Mysteries while his mouth said the words. He was disturbed one night to see Michael kneeling at the sofa saying the prayers with the Sunday paper between his elbows. Colum counted off the Hail Marys, feeding his shiny lilac rosary beads between his finger and thumb. They were really more suitable for a woman but they had come all the way from Lourdes. Where the loop of the beads joined was a little silver heart with a bubble of Lourdes water in it − like the spirit level in his brother's tool kit.

When it came to his turn to give out the prayer Colum always waited until the response was finished − not like his brothers who charged on, overlapping the prayer and the response, slurring their words to get it finished as quickly as possible. They became annoyed with him and afterwards, in whispers, accused him of being 'a creeping Jesus'.

At the end of each Rosary their mother said a special prayer 'for the Happy Repose of the Soul of Daddy'. Although he had been dead two years, it still brought a lump to Colum's throat. It wouldn't have been so bad if she had said father or something but the word Daddy made him want to cry.

Sometimes he had to go on kneeling when the others had risen to their feet in case they should see his eyes.

It was Colum's turn to do the dishes. They had their turns written up on a piece of paper so that there would be no argument. He poured some hot water into the basin from the kettle on the range. It had gone slightly brown from heating. He didn't like the look of it as much as the cold water from the pump. In the white enamel bucket under the scullery bench it looked pure and cool and still. Where the enamel had chipped off, the bucket was blue-black. If you put your hand in the water the fingers seemed to go flat.

He dipped a cup into the basin, rinsed it out and set it on the table. Father Lynch had funny fingers. He had tiny tufts of black hair on the back of each of them. They made Colum feel strange as he poured water from a cruet on to them. The priest would join his trembling index fingers and thumbs and hold them over the glass bowl, then he would take the linen cloth ironed into its folds and wipe them dry. He would put it back in its creases and lay it on Colum's arm. He had some whispered prayers to say when he was doing that. Colum always wondered why Father Lynch was so nervous saying his morning Mass. He had served for others and they didn't tremble like that. Perhaps it was because he was holier than them, that they weren't as much in awe of the Blessed Sacrament as he was. What a frightening thing it must be, to hold Christ's actual flesh — to have the responsibility to change the bread and wine into the body and blood of Jesus.

He dried the dishes and set them in neat piles before putting them back on the shelf. Above the bench Michael had fixed a small mirror for shaving. Colum had to stand on tip-toe to see himself. He was the only one of the family who had to wear glasses. He took after his father. For a long time he had to wear National Health round ones with the springy legs that hooked behind his ears, but after months of pleading and crying his mother had given in and bought him a good pair with real frames.

He went to the back door and threw out a basinful of water with a slap on to the icy ground. It steamed in the light from the scullery window. It was a still night and he could hear the children's voices yelling from the next street.

The kitchen was warm when he came back in again. Radio Luxembourg was on the wireless. Colum took all his money in his pocket and put the stubs in a brown paper bag.

'I'm away, Mammy,' he said.

She was having a cigarette, sitting with her feet up on a stool.

'Don't be late,' was all she said.

He walked a lamp post, ran a lamp post through the town until he reached the hill which led to the Parochial House. It was a large building made of the same red brick as the church. He could see lights on in the house so he climbed the hill. It was still bitterly cold and he was aware of his jaw shivering. He kept both hands in his pockets, holding the brown bag in the crook of his arm. He knocked at the door of the house. It was the priest's housekeeper who opened it a fraction. When she saw Colum she opened it wide.

'Hello, Miss Grant. Is Father Lynch in?'

'He is busy, Colum. What was it you wanted?'

'Ballot tickets, Miss. And to give in money.'

She looked over her shoulder down the hallway, then turned and put out her hand for the money.

'It's all loose, Miss,' said Colum, digging into his pocket to let her hear it.

'Oh, you'd best come in then – for a moment.'

Miss Grant brought him down the carpeted hallway to her quarters – she had a flat of her own at the back of the house. She closed the door and smiled a jumpy kind of smile – a smile that stopped in the middle. Colum emptied the bag of stubs on the table.

'There's forty-two books . . . ' he said.

'Goodness, someone has been busy.'

' . . . and here is five pounds, five shillings.' He set two pound notes and a ten shilling note on the table and handfulled the rest of the coins out of his pocket. They rang and clattered on the whitewood surface. She began to check it, scraping the coins towards her quickly and building them into piles.

'All present and correct,' she said.

Colum looked at the sideboard. There was a bottle of orange juice and a big box of biscuits which he knew was for the ticket sellers. She saw him looking.

'All right, all right,' she said.

She poured a glass of juice and allowed him to choose two biscuits. His fingers hovered over the selection.

'Oh come on, Colum, don't take all night.'

He took a chocolate one and a wafer and sat down. He had never seen Miss Grant so snappy before. Usually she was easygoing. She was very fat, with a chest like stuffed pillows under her apron. He had heard the grown-ups in the town say that if anybody had earned heaven it was her. They spoke of her goodness and kindness. 'There's one saint in that Parochial House,' they would say. For a long time Colum thought they were talking about Father Lynch.

In the silence he heard his teeth crunching the biscuit. Miss Grant did not sit down but stood by the table waiting for him to finish. He swallowed and said,

'Could I have ten more books, please?'

'Yes, dear.' She put her hands in her apron pocket and looked all around her, then left the room.

Colum had never been in this part of the house before. He had always gone into Father Lynch's room or waited in the hallway. Although it was a modern house, it was full of old things. A picture of the Assumption of Our Lady in a frame of gold leaves hung by the front door. The furniture in Father Lynch's room was black and heavy. The dining room chairs had twisted legs like barley sugar sticks. Everything had a rich feel to it, especially the thick patterned carpet. Miss Grant's quarters were not carpeted but had some rugs laid on the red tiled floor. It was the kind of floor they had at home, except that the corners of their tiles were chipped off and they had become uneven enough to trip people.

'Vera!' he heard a voice shout. It was Father Lynch.

Vera's voice answered from somewhere. Colum looked up and Father Lynch was standing in the doorway with his arm propped against the jamb.

'Hello, Father.'

'Well, if it isn't the owl,' said Father Lynch.

He wasn't dressed like a priest but was wearing an ordinary man's collarless shirt, open at the neck.

'What brings you up here, Colum?'

He moved from the door and reached out to put his hand on a chair back. Two strands of his oiled hair had come loose and fallen over his forehead. He sat down very slowly on the chair.

'Ballot tickets, Father. I've sold all you gave me.'

Father Lynch gave a loud whoop and slapped the table loudly with the flat of his hand. His eyes looked very heavy and he was blinking a lot.

'That's the way to do it. Lord, how the money rolls in.'

He was slurring his words as if he was saying the Rosary. Miss Grant came into the room holding a wad of white ballot tickets.

'Here you are now, Colum. You'd best be off.'

Colum finished his juice and stood up.

'Is that the strongest you can find for the boy to drink, Vera?' He laughed loudly. Colum had never heard him laugh before. He slapped the table again.

'Father – if you'll excuse us, I'll just show Colum out now.'

'No. No. He came to see me – didn't you?'

Colum nodded.

'He's the only one that would. Let him stay for a bit.'

'His mother will worry about him.'

'No she won't,' said Colum.

'Of course she won't,' said Father Lynch. He ignored Miss Grant. 'How many books did you sell?'

'Forty-two, Father.'

The priest raised his eyes to heaven and blew out his cheeks. Colum smelt a smell like altar wine.

'Holy Saint Christopher. Forty-two?'

'Yes.'

Miss Grant moved behind Colum and began to guide him with pressure away from the table.

'That calls for a celebration.' Father Lynch stood up unsteadily. 'Forty-two!'

He reached out to give Colum a friendly cuff on the back of the head but he missed and instead his hand struck the side of the boy's face scattering his glasses on the tiled floor.

'Aw Jesus,' said the priest. 'I'm sorry.' Father Lynch hunkered down to pick them up but lurched forward on to his knees. One lens was starred with white and the arc of the frame was broken. He hoisted himself to his feet and held the glasses close to his sagging face, looking at them.

'Jesus, I'm so sorry,' he said again. He bent down, looking for the missing piece of frame, and the weight of his head seemed to topple him. He cracked his skull with a sickening thump off the sharp edge of a radiator. One of his legs was still up in the air trying to right his balance. He put his hand to the top of his head and Colum saw that the hand was slippery with blood. Red blood was smeared from his Brylcreemed hair on to the radiator panel as the priest slid lower. His eyes were open but not seeing.

'Are you all right, Father?' Miss Grant's voice was shaking. She produced a white handkerchief from her apron pocket. The priest shouted, his voice suppressed and hissing and angry. He cursed his housekeeper and the polish on her floor. Then he raised his eyes to her without moving his head and said in an ordinary voice,

'What a mess for the boy.'

Miss Grant took the glasses which he was still clutching and put them in Colum's hand. Father Lynch began to cry with his mouth half open. Miss Grant turned the boy away and pushed him towards the door. Both she and Colum had to step over the priest to get out. She led him by the elbow down the hallway.

'That's the boy. Here's your ballot tickets.'

She opened the front door.

'Say a wee prayer for him, Colum. He's in bad need of it.'

'All right, but –'

'I'd better go back to him now.'

The door closed with a slam. Colum put his glasses on but could only see through his left eye. His knees were like water and his stomach was full of wind. He tried to get some of it up but he couldn't. He started to run. He ran all the way home. He sat panting on the cold doorstep and only went in when he got his breath back. His mother was alone.

'What happened to you? You're as white as a sheet,' she said, looking up at him. She was knitting a grey sock on three needles shaped into a triangle. Colum produced his glasses from his pocket. Within the safety of the house he began to cry.

'I bust them.'

'How, might I ask?' His mother's voice was angry.

'I was running and they just fell off. I slipped on the ice.'

'Good God, Colum, do you know how much those things cost? You'll have to get a new pair for school. Where do you think the money is going to come from? Who do you think I am, Carnegie? Eh?'

Her knitting needles were flashing and clacking. Colum continued to cry, tears rather than noise.

'Sheer carelessness. I've a good mind to give you a thumping.'

Colum, keeping out of range of her hand, sat at the table and put the glasses on. He could only half see. He put his hand in his pocket and took out his pound note.

'Here,' he said offering it to his mother. She took it and put it beneath the jug on the shelf.

'That'll not be enough,' she said, then after a while, 'Will you stop that sobbing? It's not the end of the world.'

The next morning Colum was surprised to see Father Lynch in the vestry before him. He was robed and reading his breviary, pacing the strip of carpet in the centre of the room. They said nothing to each other.

At the Consecration Colum looked up and saw the black congealed wound on the thinning crown of Father Lynch's head, as he lifted the tail of the chasuble. He saw him elevate the white disc of the host and heard him mutter the words,

'*Hoc est enim corpus meum.*'

Colum jangled the cluster of bells with angry twists of his wrist. A moment later when the priest raised the chalice full of wine he rang the bell again, louder if possible.

In the vestry afterwards he changed as quickly as he could and was about to dash out when Father Lynch called him. He had taken off his chasuble and was folding it away.

'Colum.'

'What?'

'Sit down a moment.'

He removed the cincture and put it like a coiled snake in the drawer. The boy remained standing. The priest sat down in his alb and beckoned him over.

'I'm sorry about your glasses.'

Colum stayed at the door and Father Lynch went over to him. Colum thought his face no longer sad, simply ugly.

'Your lace is loosed.' He was about to genuflect to tie it for him but Colum crouched and tied it himself. Their heads almost collided.

'It's hard for me to explain,' said Father Lynch, 'but . . . to a boy of your age sin is a very simple thing. It's not.'

Colum smelt the priest's breath sour and sick.

'Yes, Father.'

'That's because you have never committed a sin. You don't know about it.'

He removed his alb and hung it in the wardrobe.

'Trying to find the beginnings of a sin is like . . . ' He looked at the boy's face and stopped. 'Sin is a deliberate turning away from God. That is an extremely difficult thing to do. To close Him out from your love . . . '

'I'll be late for school, Father.'

'I suppose you need new glasses?'

'Yes.'

Father Lynch put his hand in his pocket and gave him some folded pound notes.

'Did you mention it to your mother?'

'What?'

'How they were broken?'

'No.'

'Are you sure? To anyone?'

Colum nodded that he hadn't. He was turning to get out the door. The priest raised his voice, trying to keep him there.

'I knew your father well, Colum,' he shouted. 'You remind me of him a lot.'

The altar-boy ran, slamming the door after him. He heard an empty wooden coat-hanger rattle on the hardboard panel of the door and it rattled in his mind until he reached the bottom of the hill. There he stopped running. He unfolded the wad of pound notes still in his hand and counted one — two — three — four of them with growing disbelief.

Eels

THE OLD WOMAN sat playing solitaire, hearing the quiet click of her wedding-ring on the polished table top each time she laid her hand flat to study the ranks of cards. They were never right. Never worked out. A crucial king face down, buried – and the game was lost. She realised how futile it was – not only this particular game but the activity of playing solitaire, and yet she could not stop herself, so she dealt the cards again. They flipped down silently, cushioned as they slid on the shine of the wood. She was reluctant to cheat. She played maybe six times before she gave up, put the cards away and sat gnawing her thumbnail. Perhaps later, left alone, it would come out.

She moved to the kitchen and took her magnesia, not bothering with the spoon but slugging the blue bottle back, hearing the white liquid tilt thickly. She swallowed hard, holding her thrapple. She stopped breathing through her nose so as not to taste, and held her mouth open. She walked to the bedroom, still breathing through her mouth until she saw herself in the mirror with crescents of white at the sides of her open lips. When she closed her teeth she heard and felt the sand of the magnesia grate between them. Her skin was loose and wrinkled, hanging about the bones she knew to be beneath her face. There were crows' feet at the corners of her eyes. With one finger she pressed down beneath her eye, baring its red sickle. They watered too much when the weather was cold. She wiped the white from the sides of her mouth with a tissue and began dressing, putting on several layers against the cold, with her old cardigan on top. She combed her white hair back from her forehead and looked at the number of hairs snagged on the comb. She removed them and with a fidget of her fingers dropped them into the waste-paper basket.

She remembered as a girl at the cottage combing her hair in spring sunshine and each day taking the dark hairs from the comb and dropping them out of the window with the same fidget of her fingers. A winter gale blew down a thrushes' nest into the garden and it was lined and snug with the black sheen of her own hair. For ages she kept it but it fell apart eventually, what with drying out and all the handling it got as she showed it to the children in class.

She lifted her raffia basket and put into it the magnesia, the pack of cards and a handful of tea-bags. In the hall she put on her heavy overcoat. The driveway to the house had not been made up, even though the house had been occupied for more than three years. It was rutted with tracks which had frozen over. She stopped to try one with the pressure of her toe, to see how heavy the frost had been. The slow ovals of bubbles separated and moved away from her toe. They returned again when she removed her weight but the ice did not break. She shuffled, afraid of falling, the ice crisping beneath her feet. Above her she saw the moon in its last phase shining at midday.

The air was bitterly cold. She had a pain in her throat which she experienced as a lump every time she swallowed. She had to chew what little she ate thoroughly or she felt it would not go past the lump. Everyone accused her of eating like a bird. Everyone said that she must see a doctor. But she knew without a doctor telling her that she would not see another winter. In September her son Brian had offered to buy her a heavy coat but she had refused, saying that she wouldn't get the wear out of it.

On the tarmac road she walked with a firmer step. There was no need to look up yet. She knew the bend, the precise gap in the hedge where she could see the lough. First she had to pass the school. The old school had been different, shaped like a church, built of white stone. But still, the new one had good toilets – better than the ones that she as a monitress had had to share with the whole school. It had got so bad that she eventually learned to hold on for the whole of the day.

The sound of the master's voice rang out impatiently as she passed, shouting a page number again and again. She smiled and anticipated the gap in the hedge. The shoulder of the hill sloped down and she raised her eyes to look at the lough. It was there, a flat bar almost to the horizon, the colour of aluminium. She stopped and stared.

Round the next turn was the cottage, set by itself with its back to the lough. No one saw her. Not that it would really matter. She let herself in the front door with her own key and hung her coat on the hall-stand beside a coat of her son's. He never wore it because he went everywhere in the car. He had got fat with lack of exercise and the modern things that Bernadette fed him. Spaghettis and curries that made the old woman's gorge rise to smell them.

In the kitchen she felt the heat on her face. She opened the door of the Rayburn so that she could see the fire and its red glow. She sank into the armchair and extended her feet to warm her shins before putting the kettle on.

From where she sat she could see the lough framed between the net curtains of the back window. When she had moved house it hadn't really occurred to her that she would miss it but the first morning when she woke she had glanced towards the window and been aware of the difference – like passing a mirror when she had had her hair cut. Then with each waking morning the loss grew. She did not become used to the field at the back. It had a drab sameness. The lough was never the same, changing from minute to minute. Now it was the colour of pewter. Through all the years she had spent in this cottage the lough was a presence. She would stand drying dishes, her eyes fixed on it but not seeing it. Making the beds, she knew it was there behind her.

Suddenly the phone rang, startling her. She looked at it, willing it to stop. She began to count the rings. At ten they should have stopped but they went on. Insistently. When they did stop they left a faint trembling echo in the silence.

She moved to fill the kettle. What if it had been an accident? At Brian's place anything could happen to him. She remembered a Saturday in Cookstown when she missed the bus and had to go round to the garage to get a lift. Brian lay in dungarees beneath a jacked-up car, speaking out to her. She hated the whole place. It was like a dark hangar, full of the smell of diesel and the echoes of dropped spanners. Rain came in through a broken sky-light and stayed in round droplets on the oily concrete. A mechanic, whistling tunelessly, started a car and revved it until she thought her head would burst. She hated the fact that Brian owned this place, but what was worse was the fact that he had bought it with money earned from fishing. Always the men of her family had fished for eels.

The kettle began a tiny rattle on the range and she took a tea-bag from her basket and put it in a cup. When the water boiled she poured it, watching it colour from yellow to mahogany. She removed the plump tea-bag with a spoon and dropped it hissing into the range. The tea clouded with the little milk she added to it.

The eels had become profitable a couple of years before her husband Hugh had died. A co-op had been formed and the prices soared. Within the space of a couple of months cracked lino was thrown out and carpet appeared in its place. They changed their van for a new car — not second-hand new. But they had worked hard for it, snatching sleep at all hours of the day and night. Often she had seen Hugh making up the lines by the light of the head-lamps – four hundred droppers with hooks off each section of line, four lines in all, while she, with her back breaking, stooped, a torch in one hand, pulling the small slippery hawsers of worms from the night ground to bait every one of them.

One night she had taken a step to the side and stood on something that made her whole head reel, something taut and soft at the same time – something living. An eel. Eels. An *ahh* of revulsion followed by 'Mother of God'. She remembered the words exactly and remembered the hair of her head being alive and rising from her scalp. She had stepped back but another squirmed under her heel. Her torch picked out the silent writhing procession, crossing the land from one water to another. Out of the depths, into the depths. Glistening like a snail's trail. Shuddering at the memory, she almost spilled her tea.

She turned on the transistor and changed the wavelength from Radio One to the local station for the news. She heard without listening, staring at the lough. Accidents, killings. The lough will claim a victim every year, was what they said. It was strange that, because on the lough there were no real storms. The water became brown and fretted when the wind got up. Even so, there were windy nights when the men were out fishing that she worried, seeing the water see-saw in the toilet bowl. Last year Hugh had died in his bed, thank God. The cat died about the same time. Both were ill for long enough.

Only once in her life had she gone out with them in the boat. When she had asked, Hugh had laughed and scorned the idea but she had said that all her life she had been cooking for them and she was curious to know what they did. Besides, now that tney had a cooker that could switch *itself* on there was no reason why she shouldn't. Every time Hugh looked at her – a spectator sitting in the prow of the boat with her arms folded – he shook his head in disbelief saying to Brian, 'As odd as two left feet.' And she knew it was a compliment. It was an open boat with an outboard and in the middle sat an oil-drum with a kitchen knife blade sharpened to a razor's edge protruding above the rim, like an Indian's feather. As the men lifted the lines, if there was an eel on, they walloped it into the drum, the blade slicing the line as they did so. She had felt a strange admiration for her husband and her son as they became involved in their work. They were so deft yet so unaware of her watching their deftness. She wanted to reach out and touch them but she knew she could not touch the thing that awed her, knew they would mock her if she tried to put it into words. She watched the writhe of brown and yellow eels build up inside the drum, intricate, ceaselessly moving, aware that each one had swallowed a hook. She was too soft, they all said. They had ridiculed her when, drowning a bagful of kittens, they caught her warming the water in the bucket to take the chill off it.

She finished her tea, swallowing hard, and while she remembered she returned the pointer on the transistor to Radio One and switched it off. It would be the kind of thing that Bernadette would notice. Always she had to leave the place exactly as she found it. One day when she had been on one of her 'visits' she had seen a young man crouching outside the garden gate at the back. She was not afraid but curious. As an excuse she had hung out a dish-towel and asked him what he was doing.

'I'm a student – of a sort. I'm looking at rocks.'

He had a bag over his shoulder and a hammer in his hand. She offered him a cup of tea and he accepted. He was young and full of an enthusiasm for learning that her own son lacked. But he had tried to talk down to her, using simple words to explain the geological research he was engaged in. She told him curtly that she had been a teacher.

'The latest theory,' he said, 'is that the continents are moving. These vast countries can move vast distances. But it takes a vast time.'

'I'm vastly impressed,' she said. 'More tea?'

He held out his cup by the handle and she filled it. His skin was pale and he had not shaved for several days, but his eyes were keen.

'Can you imagine it,' he said, 'that South America and Africa were once joined together? And now they are thousands of miles apart? The evidence is in the rocks. Think of the power.'

He set down his cup and slid one hand heavily over the other.

'Yes,' she said.

As they talked the boy smoked a lot of cigarettes, each time offering her one, which she refused. She asked him if he was married and he told her that he was engaged to a girl from Cookstown. After he graduated they would get married. To her surprise the old woman did not know her name or any of her connection when he said it. It was a changed place, Cookstown.

After he had gone she brought in the dish-towel and flapped it in front of the open window to clear the house of smoke. Bernadette had a sharp nose, which she wrinkled at any smell. She also detested the way her daughter-in-law held her shoulders high as she worked about the house — the clipped way she spoke, as if to say, 'I'll talk to you but I have my work to get on with.' Old before her years, that one. The house was perfect anyway, without chick nor child to untidy it. One of the things that had annoyed her most was the speed with which Bernadette had redecorated the cottage when they had moved out to the new bungalow. She couldn't have lived with the walls as they were, she said, giving that little shrug of her spiky shoulders.

The old woman moved to the table at the window and

began a game of solitaire. The lough had become the colour of lead. She looked at the sky, now overcast. The snap-up roller blind was stuck all over with long-legged midges. They came in clouds in the summer and, like a smell, couldn't be kept out by shutting doors or windows. She dealt quickly, the cards making a flacking noise as they came off the deck. Solitaire annoyed Bernadette. She thought it a waste of time. The old woman *knew* it was. All her life she had wanted to halt the time passing but she never felt like that until *afterwards*. She was either too busy or too tired to capture and hold the moment. Brian was now married and loosened his trousers after a meal. How long ago was it that she had taken his two ankles between the trident of her fingers to position him on his nappy? Or used egg-white to stiffen and hold in place the flap of hair that fell over his eyes before he had his first communion photograph taken? Or nudged him in his stained suit to the bedroom and let him lean his head on her shoulder while she fumbled at the laces of his shoes and became white with anger and fear that he had driven the van home in such a condition? Like everyone else, she had applauded at his wedding.

Jack on queen and she was stuck. There was nothing else to move and she pulled the cards towards her with a sigh of exasperation. She rose to go to the bathroom. As she climbed the stairs she put a hand on each thigh and pushed. There was a time when she could have bounded up them two at a time. In the bathroom the toilet-roll was olive green and went almost black in the bowl. She wandered the bedrooms, not recognising them as her own. The neatness, the colours. The view from the window had not changed. This was the room where she had given birth to Brian. The only detail she remembered from that night was the crackling of newspaper beneath her. To this day she couldn't bear to sit on a newspaper, even if it was beneath the cushion.

Downstairs she made another cup of tea and ate a dry

biscuit, massaging it past her thrapple the way she had seen the vet help pills down the cat's throat. She found that it went down easier if she put her head back in the chair . . .

She woke in panic. It was dark and the rain was rattling against the window. For a moment she did not know where she was, thought the cottage was her own again. She switched on the table lamp and looked at the clock — a quarter past five. She began to gather her stuff. She washed the cup and returned it to its hook. She hadn't realised that it had been so late. As quickly as she was able she damped down the fire with slack and closed it up. Some spilled from the shovel on to the lino with a rattle and she cursed herself for her carelessness. She swept it in beneath the range.

Outside it was moonless dark and still raining but the cold of the morning had disappeared. The cottage was silent after the echoing slam of the door except for the gurgling of water in the gratings.

Behind the hill she saw the white fan of a car's headlights, then the electric glare as it broke the horizon. She watched it come towards the cottage. It slowed down and indicated before the lane end. Quickly she slipped through the gap in the hedge into the field. The car splashed and bounced through the pot-holes up the track. Unable to crouch much, the old woman put her neck forward and lowered her head. They must have left early. The cottage flooded with light. She heard Bernadette's voice, complaining as usual, say,

'You don't expect me to carry this weight, do you?'

The front door banged shut. The old woman stood in the field trembling.

'And what makes you so different?' she said. They were the first words she had spoken since Tuesday and they made the bones of her head vibrate. The moon was in its last phase and she felt the rain on the backs of her hands. Her tremble turned to nausea and panic and she shuddered. On such a night the eels would be moving through the grass. Her hair became live. She had seen Hugh's finger once when bitten by an eel, the bone like mother-of-pearl through the wound. Tensing the arches of her feet, she stepped awkwardly through the gap in the hedge. In the lane she kept to the side, avoiding the pot-holes. Somewhere a procession of eels would be writhing towards the lough. Out of the depths, into the depths. She turned her head and looked to see the water. She saw nothing but blackness, an infinity rising unbroken in an arch above her head.

Now as she looked at the cottage backed by darkness with its yellow windows reflected in the puddles, and in the knowledge that somewhere not too far away the earth was alive with eels – at that moment she knew her life was over. It hadn't come out. Not the way she wanted. She was aware of the lump in her throat and knew that her eyes were full of water. Beneath her feet continents were moving. She put her head down into the slanting rain and began the slow walk to the bungalow, her coat unbuttoned.

Language, Truth and Lockjaw

NORMAN SAT IN the dentist's waiting room. Outside, the rain needled down from a grey sky. The wet shining roofs descended like steps to the sea. Because he was an emergency he had to wait for over an hour while people with appointments filed past him.

Then the dentist's bespectacled head appeared round the door and said,

'Mr Noyes?'

There were two dentists on the island and it was immediately obvious to Norman that he had picked the wrong one. As he called out his secret codes to his assistant he breathed halitosis. He dug into the molar that was causing the trouble and Norman yelled, his voice breaking embarrassingly.

'That seems to be the one,' said the dentist. 'I don't think we can save it. It's a whited sepulchre.'

He went to the window and filled a large syringe. Before he approached the chair he considerately hid it behind his back.

'Open up,' he said. 'That should go dead in a minute. On holiday?'

'Yes.'

'The weather has been poor.'

159

'You can say that again.'

He had known from the minute the trip had been proposed that everything would go wrong. Patricia said that he had helped in no small measure to *make* it go wrong by his bloody-minded attitude. When *she* was a child on holiday her father, when it rained, had dressed them up in bathing suits and wellies and Pakamacs and taken them for riotous walks along the beach. He had litten — her own word — blue smoke fires with damp driftwood. But now when it rained he, Norman, retreated to the bedroom with his books. His defence was that he had work to do and that he had agreed to the trip only on condition that he could finish his paper on Ryle.

'What do you do?' asked the dentist.

'I teach. Lecturing at the University.'

'Oh. What in?'

'Philosophy.'

'That's nice.'

Things were beginning to happen in his jaw like pins and needles.

'Where are you staying?'

'We have a bungalow up at Ard-na-something.'

'Oh yes. Beside the old Mansion House. Interesting neighbours.'

Norman supposed he was referring to the mentally handicapped men he had seen staring at him over the wall. They stood for hours in the rain, immobile as sentries, watching the house. At night he heard hooting laughter and yelps and howls which previously he had only associated with a zoo.

'Open wide.' He hung a suction device like a walking stick in Norman's mouth. 'Relax now. Sometimes I think it would be better to hook that thing down the front of your trousers. Some patients sweat more than they salivate.'

The assistant smiled. She was plain but from where he lay Norman could see that the middle button of her white coat was undone and he could just see the underslope of her breast in a lacy bra.

The dentist leaned on Norman's bottom jaw and began working inside his mouth. There was a cracking sound and the dentist tut-tutted and went to a cupboard behind the chair. He's broken it, thought Norman.

'How long are you here for?' asked the dentist.

'A ort igh.'

'That's nice.'

'I cank cose i jaw.'

'What?'

Norman pointed to his lower jaw making foolish noises.

'Oh,' said the dentist. He manipulated the jaw and clicked it back into place. 'The muscle must be weak.'

'Is it broken – the tooth?'

'No, it's out.'

Norman was astonished. He had felt nothing.

Patricia shouted out from the kitchen.

'Well, love, how did it go?'

Norman had to step over the children, who were playing with a brightly coloured beach-ball on the carpet of the hallway. Although it was five o'clock on a summer's afternoon the light had to be switched on.

'O.K. He pulled it.' Norman produced a Kleenex with its soggy red spot and offered it to his wife. She refused to look at it, telling him to throw it in the bin. She asked,

'Did you expect something from the fairies for it?'

'I just thought you might be interested, that's all.'

'Aww you poor thing,' she said, kissing him lightly on the cheek. 'Did you feel that? Perhaps I should kiss you on the side that's not numb.' She had a levity and a patronising approach to him in sickness which he did not like.

'I think I'll lie down for a while. One *ought* to after an extraction.'

'Whatever you say. Will you want something to eat?'

'What are you making?'

'Spaghetti.'

'We'll see.'

In the bedroom he kicked off his shoes and stood at the rain-spotted window. They were there again, standing amongst the trees at the wall. Their heads were just visible, hair plastered wet and flat. After enquiring at the shop they had found out that the Mansion House was a holiday home for the region and that a party of mentally retarded men was staying there. A mixture of mongols and cretins and God knows what. When they saw Norman appear at the window they faded back into the trees.

He lay down on the bed and got beneath the coverlet. The room smelled damp. It had probably been empty over the summer months as well as the winter. Who in their right mind would want to stay beside a madhouse? He closed his eyes and his left ear began to whine like a high-pitched siren in the distance. He wondered if this was normal. With relief he heard the noise fade as his ear tingled back to ordinary sensation. He knew he was a hypochondriac. At night when he couldn't sleep, usually after working on a lecture or a paper, he would become aware of his heart-thud and lie awake waiting for it to miss. A discomfort in his arm, in time, would become a definite pain and a symptom of an impending heart attack. A discomfort anywhere else in his body would lead to thoughts of cancer. Laziness could be mistaken for debility, which would become a sure sign of leukaemia. This laziness could last for days and gave him much to worry about.

Although he did not say these things out loud somehow Patricia knew his nature and treated him in an off-hand way like a child. Before he married her she had been a primary school teacher and there was always a hint of it in the way she talked to him when he was ill or said he was feeling unwell.

She had spotted the medical dictionary he had slipped in among his other books to be taken on holiday but he had made an excuse, saying that in remote places, like an island off the Scottish coast, anything could happen to her or the kids. She had pointed out to him that there was an air-ambulance service straight to the nearest fully equipped hospital on the mainland at any time of the day or night. At his insistence she had checked with the tourist board by phone that this was so.

Without articulating it they both knew that they had reached a stale point in their nine-year-old marriage. They no longer talked or argued as they once did and sarcasm coloured most of the things they said to one another.

Each year they went to the same place for a month's holiday along with other families they knew. In March Norman had been sitting reading the paper when Patricia said,

'I think we should go away for a holiday just by ourselves.'

'What about the children?'

'Oh, we would take *them*.'

'How can we be by ourselves if the children are there?'

'It would get us away from the same old faces. The same old interminable conversations. Get away somewhere isolated. We would be by ourselves at night.'

'But I have this paper to finish . . . .'

'You're at the sports page already,' she squawked and fell about laughing. It was something which had endeared her to him when they first met, but now after ten years of knowing her it was something he couldn't understand — how something she considered funny seemed to take over her whole body and flop it about. One night at a party someone had told her a joke and she had slid down the wall, convulsing and spilling her drink in jerking slops on the floor. In the morning when he asked her she couldn't remember what the joke was about.

His tendency was to smile, a humour of the mind, some-

163

thing witty rather than funny affected him. There were times when the company about him were in fits of laughter and he couldn't see the joke.

The children in the hallway began to fight, then one of them broke into a howl of tears. Norman turned his good ear to the pillow. Children, especially of their age, were totally irrational. The younger was Becky, a gap-toothed six-year-old who refused to eat anything which was good for her and insisted on everything which was sweet and bad. John was two years older and had his mother's loud sense of humour. At least he ate cauliflower. He must have fallen asleep because the children wakened him with whispers, creeping round the bed.

'Mum says tea,' they shouted, seeing him awake.

Norman got up. His mouth tasted awful and he washed what remained of his teeth ruefully with peppermint toothpaste, thinking about old age. He sucked some spaghetti into the unaffected side of his mouth and crushed it carefully with his tongue against the roof of his mouth.

'How do you feel now, dear?' asked Patricia.

'So-so,' he said, 'I think the dentist must have served his time in an abattoir. My jaw is sore.'

'Look, Mum, there they are again,' said Becky.

'Who, dear?'

'The loonies.'

'So they are, God love them,' said Patricia.

Norman looked over his shoulder out of the dining room window. They were standing at the wall again, six of them. They had moved from the bedroom to the dining room. When they saw Norman turn his head they ducked down, then slowly came up again. The one who stood with his mouth hanging open shouted something unintelligible and the others laughed.

'You shouldn't call them loonies,' said Norman.

'Spacers, then,' said John.

'You shouldn't call them that either.'

'That's what they are, isn't it?'

Norman looked at his wife.

'I suppose it didn't mention this fact in the brochure for the house?'

'No, dear, it didn't. Four minutes from the beach was enough for me. Shall I pull the blind for you?'

'No, but it's something animal in me. I don't like to be watched while I'm eating.'

'It's good to know there's some animal in you.'

Norman gave her a look then switched his gaze to his son.

'John, is that the way to hold your fork?'

The rest of the evening the children spent watching the black and white television set which they had scorned when they first arrived. Norman went to the bedroom to do some work. He was writing a paper sparked off by Ryle's distinction between pleasure and pain – that they were not elements on the same spectrum, that positive quantities of one did not lead to minus quantities of the other. He had become involved in tortuous arguments about sadism and masochism. He had shown his draughts to the Prof who had said, after some consideration, that the paper was tending more to the physiological than the philosophic. He had added, looking over his glasses, that he much preferred a wank. 'Marriage is all right,' he had said, 'but there's nothing like the real thing.'

Norman never knew how to take him, never knew when he was serious. The man could be guilty of the most infantile jokes. He repeatedly accused Norman of talking a lot of hot Ayer and of being easily Ryled. What could you say to a man like that? He was always goosing and patting his young secretary – and she didn't seem to mind. He was a woolly existentialist who spoke about metaphysical concepts that could not be defined. He said that, with its pernickety approach to language, British philosophy was disappearing up its own arse while the world around it was in chaos. Also that British philosophy – including Norman – was like a butcher sharpening his knives. Eventually the knives would wear away but the meat would still be there to be cut. Norman thought, what more could you expect from the son of a County Derry farmer?

Norman had just written the first sentence of the severe rewriting the Prof had suggested when Patricia came into the room.

'Norman, the rain's gone off. Let's go for a walk.'

'But the writing is just beginning to go well.'

She put her arms around his neck.

'Don't be so solemn. It has stopped piddling for the first time since we arrived. There is even some blue in the sky. Come for a walk to the pier with us.'

Outside, the light had an eerie translucent quality. It was about ten o'clock and the low white sun had come through the cloud out over the Atlantic and was highlighting the gable ends of houses. The road was still wet and shining. The children in anoraks ran on ahead, leaving Norman and Patricia walking together.

'How's the toofy-peg?' Patricia asked.

'How is its absence, you mean.'

'Well, if you insist.'

'Not too bad now.'

'As night approaches.'

'You could put it that way.' He smiled. 'What do you think?'

'Yes. Holidays I feel like it more often.'

'Tomorrow this socket will begin to heal – usually that's bad news. Isn't it funny how you can never smell your own breath?'

He reached out and took her by the hand. Her face showed mock surprise but she responded by squeezing his fingers.

'Of course we don't have to kiss,' he said, smiling.

'Like an egg without salt. A total perversion.'

She leaned over and kissed him as they walked. They stopped in the middle of the road and kissed mouth to mouth lightly, friendly. John whistled *wheet-weeo* at them from a distance and they laughed. Norman was much taller than she and it was easy for him to put his arm around her shoulder as they walked.

At eleven Patricia turned on the ancient electric blanket at its highest – it had gears, almost, instead of settings – to try to get rid of the damp smell. Norman was reading a journal by the fire. She sat opposite him, her hands empty. A grandfather clock ticked loudly in the corner.

'One of the ideas of this holiday was that we should talk,' she said.

'Uh-huh.' He turned the page.

'You don't talk to me any more.'

'I'm sorry, what's that?'

'We don't talk any more.'

He closed the journal with a smile but kept his place with a finger.

'O.K. What would you like to talk about?'

'Anything.'

The grandfather clock worked itself up to a long whirr before striking a quarter past.

'The more I think of it,' began Norman, 'the more I am convinced that there might be something in what the Prof says – that British philosophy is trying to commit hara-kiri. And I'm not sure that that is such a good thing. I would hate to end up believing the same things as that man.'

'I would like to talk about us. What we think, what we feel.'

'Hard words, Trish. "Think" and "feel". It's difficult to know what we mean by them. It's essential that we get our concepts straight.'

'Bollocks, Norman. Let's talk about something else.'

'Why? You said we could talk about anything.'

'O.K.' She thought for a moment, then said. 'Those people who stare over the wall. Do you think because they are less intelligent they have less vivid emotions?'

'What are "vivid" emotions?'

'You know what I mean.'

'Seriously I don't.'

'The kind of thing you find in Lawrence.'

'That man is a fog of urges. He's groping all the time — making up words. Blood consciousness; the dark forest of the human soul. Patricia, if you can't put a thing into language, it doesn't exist.'

'Norman, what utter . . .'

'To answer your question. It's a problem for physiologists or neurologists or somebody like that. I don't know what loonies feel.'

'It's no wonder we don't talk any more.'

'Why's that?'

'Because you talk such utter balls. That someone should dismiss Lawrence with a wave of . . .'

'Trish.'

'What?'

'Trish. Let's have a cup of tea and go to bed. Arguing will put us off. You can't make love when you're seething. Besides this tooth of mine is beginning to hurt.'

'Absence of tooth.'

'O.K. If we sit up much longer you'll go sleepy on me.'

Patricia sighed and made a cup of tea while Norman finished reading the article in his journal.

'It's a good question,' he said, softening his biscuit in his tea and sucking it into the good side of his mouth, 'but I honestly don't know the answer to it. Taken logically it would mean that the most intelligent men have the — as you call them — the most vivid emotional responses. That is obviously not true.'

'Not in your case anyway.' She smiled or sneered at him, he couldn't tell which because he only caught the end of it.

'But I thought we weren't going to argue.'

On holidays they had agreed to do equal shares of the housework. It was Norman's turn to wash the cups, which he did even though he had had a tooth out. While he was in the kitchen Patricia took a burning peat from the fire with a pair of tongs and incensed the bedroom.

'I love that smell,' she said. 'Do you want to come to bed now?'

'I'll just wait till the smoke clears.'

As he slowly dried the cups and tidied up, his tongue sought out the jellied cavity and he touched and tasted its coppery acidity. There was no pain in it now. Perhaps he was a better dentist than he gave him credit for. Just in case he took three Disprin dissolved in water before he locked up and turned out the lights.

In the bedroom Patricia lay reading with her bare arms outside the counterpane. Her hair was undone. A strange ululating cry came from the direction of the Mansion House. Norman looked out between the drawn curtains, half expecting to see six heads lined up at the windowsill to watch, but the Mansion House was in darkness. The sound, like a child's version of a long Red Indian war cry, came again, chilling him.

'Woolawoolawoolawoolawoolawoolwoola.'

'God, what a place.'

He undressed and slipped in naked beside her nakedness. She was still a beautiful woman and, although he had come to know her body, he never ceased to be awed by it in total nakedness. She told him how aroused she was. A simple thing like holding hands earlier in the evening had been the start of it. Her voice was hushed. Her arousal touched him and they made love. Because of his condition he suggested that she did not put her tongue in his mouth. Nevertheless, Norman got the feeling that this was good sex in this strange, lightly creaking bed. When they came together he made an involuntary animal noise far back in his throat and his mouth fell wide open.

'Agggghrrrrr,' he said.

The noise he made was followed by an audible click. Patricia, with her eyes closed, was listening to her own breathing subside and touching his shoulders with her fingertips. She opened her eyes and looked at him. His mouth was open and his eyes were staring wide in fright.

'i aws gust,' said Norman.

'What?'

'i aw. It's gust.'

Patricia began to laugh, shaking and cupping her ear to him as if she couldn't hear properly.

'What are you saying?'

Norman pointed to his yawning mouth and said as clearly as he was able,

'ock jaw.'

'I thought you were having a heart attack.'

Now that she understood she advised him with amused concern that the best thing he could do in the circumstances would be to get off her. Norman struggled into a pair of pyjama bottoms and regarded himself in the mirror. He kept trying to close his mouth but nothing happened. Somewhere in his jaw the circuits had fused again. Over his shoulder he saw his wife's reflection sitting up in bed heaving in suppressed bare-breasted laughter. When he turned to face her with his mouth agape her laughter became sound. Loud, whinnying and vulgar.

'Oh Norman, you look so *stupid*. You're like one of the loonies,' she managed to say between wheezes. 'Are you kidding me?'

He turned away from her and tried to remember what the dentist had done. He took his lower jaw in his left hand and pushed. Nothing happened. He tried to push upwards and sideways and sideways and downwards but with no effect.

Patricia had put on her nightdress and was now standing looking at him in the mirror. She turned him and looked into his mouth.

'You look like the man in the moon,' she said, giggling. She tried to put it back into place. He had to bend his knees to let her reach up and he had his arms hanging loose by his sides. Patricia stepped back and looked at him, then subsided into peals of laughter again. 'Better still. One of those monkey moneyboxes.' She clapped her hands. 'You put a penny in his hand and he went – gulp.' She demonstrated. 'We had one with its jaw broken.' Norman turned away from her and scrabbled about in the cardboard box of his philosophy books until he found his medical dictionary. He wondered what heading would be the most helpful to read. With his jaw locked open he couldn't swallow his saliva and it drooled over his bottom lip on to the page. He pored over the book.

'anky.'

Patricia gave him a handkerchief from the open case on the dresser and he staunched his dribbles.

'I'm getting to interpret your grunts quite well,' she said. Norman could find nothing which related to his case except under tetanus which he was fairly sure he didn't have. He thought of going to the square and phoning from a callbox for the ambulance plane, until he remembered that he couldn't even speak and they would think he was drunk. Patricia would have to do it. He imagined arriving alone in the infirmary at Glasgow or somewhere in his pyjama bottoms and trying with gestures and groans to explain the complexities of what had happened. With great difficulty he told his wife the thought.

'If you're going out,' she said wiping the tears from her cheeks, 'we'll have to put a coffee-tin lid in your mouth to keep the draught out.' She fell on the bed and rolled about. 'You're agog,' she shrieked. 'Agog describes you perfectly. Norman, you're the perfection of agogness.'

'or ucks ake Trish,' he said, 'ee serious.'

The noise from the Mansion House came again, ridiculing him.

'Woolawoolawoolawoolawoolawoola.'

Patricia was by now as inarticulate as he was. She was becoming almost hysterical and Norman, even in the midst of his trouble, wondered if he should slap her face to bring her out of it. It was obviously a nervous reaction to what had happened. As if he didn't have enough to cope with.

He went to the bathroom to see if a change of mirror would help. Sexual pleasure had reduced him to a slavering moron. He thought of D. H. Lawrence and Patricia's admiration for him. He pulled and pushed and wiggled at his bottom jaw. He looked and felt like the mental defectives who had peered at him over the wall. To be like this for ever. In the distance the grandfather clock tolled midnight. He had been like this for the best part of half an hour. He would *have* to go to hospital. There was the dentist but he didn't know where he lived. He didn't even know his name. Then suddenly he remembered that the Prof's wife had been a practising dentist at one time. He could phone him long distance and ask her advice. Again he remembered that he couldn't speak. It would only give the Prof another chance to say, 'Noyes, you're full of sound and fury signifying nothing.' The bastard.

All Patricia's squawking and hooting had wakened John and he came, puffy-faced with sleep, to the bathroom. He peed, forgot to flush it and walked past his father as he stared in the mirror.

'Hunggh,' said Norman. The boy turned. Norman pointed to the lavatory.

'What?'

'uh it.'

The child stood not understanding, holding up his pyjama trousers by the loose waist. Norman took him by the shoulders and led him back to the lavatory. A little saliva spilled on to John's head and Norman rubbed it.

'uh it.'

'Daddy, what's wrong?'

Norman lifted the child's hand and rested it on the handle – then pressed both hand and handle. The lavatory flushed noisily and the child staggered sleepily back to his bedroom.

'What's wrong with Daddy?' Norman heard him ask in the hallway.

'He's having a long yawn, dear. Now go back to bed.'

Patricia came in with the medical dictionary opened at a page.

'Look, this is it,' she said pointing to a diagram, 'down and out and *then* up. Here, let me try.'

She set the book on the Vanitory unit, stood on tip-toe, still consulting it over her shoulder, and took his jaw firmly in her hands. She pulled downwards and towards herself. Norman agghed and she pushed hard. There was a gristle-snapping sound and his mouth closed. He tried it tentatively, partially opening and closing it, like a goldfish.

'You've done it,' he said. He wiggled it laterally just to make sure. 'I was imagining all kinds of terrible things.' He laughed nervously.

'But you looked *so* funny, Norman. I'm sorry for laughing.' Her shoulders were still shaking.

'You have a strange sense of humour.' He wiped the shine

off his chin with the handkerchief. 'The next time I get my foreskin caught in my zip I'll let you know and we can have a night's entertainment.

Back in the bedroom Patricia imitated a chimpanzee with her mouth open and arms dangling and said,

'Poor Norm.'

When they were settled in bed he sighed.

'I thought I was a goner. The dentist says I must have a weak muscle.'

'There's nothing wrong with your muscle, darling,' she said and snuggled in to his side. The fine rain had begun again and he heard it hiss off the roof and the surrounding trees. He would never understand this crazy woman he was married to. It was hurtful to be laughed *at*. But he was grateful to her for putting his jaw back and, in a kind of thanksgiving, he resolved to take the whole family for a walk along the beach the next day to light bonfires, whether it rained or not.

He turned out the light. The yelling from the Mansion House seemed to have stopped but he couldn't be sure it would not begin again. In the dark, as they were drifting off to sleep, Patricia shook the bed with giggles in the same way as shudders remain after a long bout of crying.

BY BERNARD MAC LAVERTY
ALSO AVAILABLE IN VINTAGE

☐	CAL	£5.99
☐	GRACE NOTES	£6.99
☐	THE GREAT PROFUNDO	£5.99
☐	SECRETS	£5.99
☐	WALKING THE DOG	£6.99

- All Vintage books are available through mail order or from your local bookshop.

- Please send cheque/eurocheque/postal order (sterling only), Access, Visa, Mastercard, Diners Card, Switch or Amex:

☐☐☐☐☐☐☐☐☐☐☐☐☐☐☐☐

Expiry Date:_____ Signature:_____

Please allow 75 pence per book for post and packing U.K.
Overseas customers please allow £1.00 per copy for post and packing.

ALL ORDERS TO:
Vintage Books, Books by Post, TBS Limited, The Book Service,
Colchester Road, Frating Green, Colchester, Essex CO7 7DW

NAME:_____

ADDRESS:_____

_____

_____

Please allow 28 days for delivery. Please tick box if you do not ☐
wish to receive any additional information
Prices and availability subject to change without notice.